Wil Usdi

AMERICAN INDIAN LITERATURE AND CRITICAL STUDIES SERIES

Colonel William Holland Thomas (Wil Usdi), 1858.
Courtesy of The State Archives of North Carolina, Albert Barden Photographic Collection.

WIL USDI

Thoughts from the Asylum,

a Cherokee Novella

Robert J. Conley

Foreword by Luther Wilson

WITH A TRIBUTE BY MICHELL HICKS

UNIVERSITY OF OKLAHOMA PRESS ◆ NORMAN

Lines from the Song of Solomon 2:2–3 (KJV) are quoted in chapter 5, page 44.

Lines from William Shakespeare, *The Tragedy of King Lear,* edited and revised by Ebenezer Charlton Black (Boston: Ginn & Co., 1911), are quoted in chapter 7: 3.4.12–14, 21–22 appear on page 61; 3.2.1–9 are on page 60; and 3.2. 14, 19–20, 24 are on page 61.

Lines from William Shakespeare, *Hamlet: Prince of Denmark*, edited by W. G. Clark and W. A. Wright, 2nd ed. (Oxford: Clarendon, 1878), are quoted in chapters 9 and 11: 3.1.64–68 appear on page 75; and 1.2.133–37 are on page 92.

Four lines from Samuel Taylor Coleridge, *The Rime of the Ancient Mariner* (New York: D. Appleton & Co., 1857), are quoted in chapter 12 and appear on page 103.

Library of Congress Cataloging-in-Publication Data
Conley, Robert J., author.
Wil Usdi: thoughts from the asylum, a Cherokee novella / Robert J. Conley.
    pages   cm.—
(American Indian literature and critical studies series; Volume 64)
ISBN 978-0-8061-4659-1 (pbk.: alk. paper)
1. Cherokee Indians—Fiction. 2. Historical fiction. I. Title.
PS3553.O494W476 2015
813'.54—dc23

2014032931

Wil Usdi: Thoughts from the Asylum, a Cherokee Novella is Volume 64 in the American Indian Literature and Critical Studies Series.

The paper in this book meets the guidelines for permanence and durability of the Committee on Production Guidelines for Book Longevity of the Council on Library Resources, Inc. ∞

1 2 3 4 5 6 7 8 9 10

Contents

Foreword

Luther Wilson

If there were such a position as Official Cherokee Historian, Robert J. Conley would be the logical choice to hold that position. In *The Cherokee Nation: A History* (University of New Mexico Press, 2008), Conley wrote the best general narrative history of the Cherokee Nation published in the past one hundred years. In addition, Conley's multivolume fiction masterpiece, The Real People series, published by St. Martin's Press and the University of Oklahoma Press, is collectively the most complete, most accurate, and most readable history of the Cherokees ever written. Beginning with *The Way of the Priests* and continuing on through at least twelve volumes, Conley writes of the trials, tribulations, and triumphs of the Cherokee People. *Publishers Weekly* described Conley's *War Woman,* a particular volume in the series, as "a lively, informed piece of speculative history." Conley has told the Cherokees' stories in poetry, prose, fiction, and at least one drama, *Mountain Windsong,* which is adapted from his novel of the same title and portrays the realities of the Trail of Tears—the tragic and wilfully malign removal of the Cherokee people from their ancestral homelands in the Southeast to their new homes in what is now northeastern Oklahoma.

Conley also wrote several fictionalized biographies of key individuals important to Cherokee history, including *Sequoyah* and

Ned Christie's War. This new novella, *Wil Usdi: Thoughts from the Asylum*, is one of those fictionalized biographies. William Holland Thomas, born in 1805 near present-day Waynesville, North Carolina, was also known as Wil Usdi (Little Will), the name given him by his adoptive Cherokee father, Yonaguska (Thomas's white father drowned before he was born). When Thomas was around the age of twelve, his mother decided it was time he struck out on his own, so she sent him off to apprentice himself for three years to Felix Walker, a trader who worked among the Cherokees in western North Carolina.

Homeschooled by his mother, Thomas was a bright and personable young man who was proficient in both spoken and written English. Through his work with Walker among the Cherokees, he became fluent in both spoken and written Cherokee as well. Shortly after beginning to work at one of Walker's trading posts, Thomas met Yonaguska (Drowning Bear), a highly respected man among his Cherokee clans. Yonaguska was so impressed with the young man that he adopted him as his son.

At the end of Thomas's apprenticeship, Walker confessed that he was broke and could not pay Wil (as he was known then) for his work. He gave Thomas instead his remaining trade goods and several volumes of old law books. Thanks to Thomas's ability to communicate in Cherokee and through the support among the Cherokees of his adoptive father, Yonaguska, Wil became a very successful trader and one of the wealthiest men in western North Carolina. He learned law from his books and used that knowledge successfully in his business affairs. He also used his expertise to help the people who would become the Eastern Band of Cherokees to remain in their ancestral lands in North Carolina at the time when most other Cherokees were being rounded up by Andrew Jackson's troops and herded off on the Trail of Tears to present-day northeastern Oklahoma.

Over the next couple of decades leading up to the Civil War, Thomas became a successful and highly respected politician in North Carolina, and at Yonaguska's urging he successfully represented the Eastern Band of Cherokees in Washington, D.C. He helped win many Cherokee claims against the government for annuity payments, and he used those funds along with his personal funds to buy more than 50,000 acres of land. By 1860, that land, combined with ongoing purchases, became known as the Qualla Boundary. It is now the core of the present-day Eastern Band of Cherokees.

Thomas followed much of the remainder of the South and joined the Confederacy in the Civil War. He organized more than four hundred members of the Eastern Cherokees into a Confederate Legion of Cherokees. The legion served mostly in eastern Tennessee, protecting important bridges from being burned by Union troops and civilian Union sympathizers. The legion finally saw some regular military action in Waynesville, North Carolina, at the end of the war. After the war, Thomas's businesses and personal finances were in ruins and his health began to fail. He spent most of the remainder of his life in the mental health hospitals in Morganton and Raleigh, North Carolina, which, ironically, he had helped establish with funds from the North Carolina Legislature while serving as a senator from western North Carolina.

Conley lets Thomas tell his fascinating story mostly from the perspective of his confinement in the mental hospital. It is a sad, poignant, and sometimes uplifting story as Thomas struggles with his failing memory to reconstruct his remarkably illustrious past. During occasional periods of remission, he is released to return home to his wife, children, and old friends; but these times are brief, and the ravages of the war and his failing memory send him back to the confines of the hospital. In the end it is a tragic story for Thomas but a triumphant story for the Eastern Band of Cherokees, who, thanks in large part to Thomas's efforts on their behalf, remain today on their ancestral homelands. The U.S. government, never in a rush to pay reparations and make right previous misguided actions, eventually allowed the Cherokees to hold land titles in their own names; and in 1882, the U.S. Supreme Court declared the Eastern Band of Cherokees a legitimate tribe.

Conley paints a story to be savored, a deeply empathetic portrait of Wil Usdi and of the Eastern Band of Cherokees who, thanks in great part to Thomas's efforts on their behalf, survived the most disruptive times in their history. They now live and prosper in their beautiful homeland on the eastern edge of the Great Smoky Mountains.

A Tribute from the Eastern Band of Cherokee Indians

Michell Hicks

PRINCIPAL CHIEF OF THE EASTERN
BAND OF CHEROKEE INDIANS

William Holland Thomas has long held a place of honor among our people, but what we know of his life is a blend of fact and fiction. He is often referred to as the white Chief, as though our friendship with him was valid only if he held that title. Robert J. Conley has used this novella to dispel that myth and to capture what the Cherokee people in North Carolina truly felt for Wil Usdi.

Robert's heart shines through in this work, and the Cherokee point of view he portrays is uncanny. The history of our people is often told through the work of historians with little understanding of our community. Robert brings us into the complex life of the Eastern Cherokees during a tumultuous time. Wil Usdi gives me a better understanding of the people who worked diligently to shape the life I now have. Rarely has a work of fiction provided me an understanding of the humanity of our people, our friends, and our neighbors, who were responsible both for protecting our right to exist as a distinct nation of people and for diminishing our culture.

Robert follows a great tradition of Cherokee writers in bringing to light those aspects of our community that are most dear to our hearts, and he utilizes a platform that speaks to Cherokee people and those who want to know us better. Robert's mastery of the written word continues a long Cherokee tradition of memo-rializing not only our thoughts but, more importantly, our feel-ings. This work in particular captures the essence of acceptance inside a closed Cherokee community during a time of suspicion and mistrust.

The community of the Eastern Band of Cherokee Indians was shaped by and through the life of William Holland Thomas, and this novella is a fitting tribute to his legacy. Wil Usdi is also important to the legacy of our people because it follows in the tradition of Cherokee writers and thinkers. Robert stands out as an important writer in America and as a significant Cherokee voice. Our people have depended on Cherokee visionaries, like Robert, to celebrate our survival through the good times and the bad. He creates a human Cherokee world for the reader to become part of and to leave with a human experience.

Throughout his long writing career, Robert J. Conley has worked to create a visual image of our people and I believe this work is a fitting end to a life well lived. I am honored to have crossed paths with him, and honored to have experienced his vision of the life of Wil Usdi.

Preface

William Holland Thomas was an important man in western North Carolina history. He was born in 1805 near what is now Waynesville, North Carolina, and at age twelve or thirteen went to work among the Cherokees as a storekeeper for a man who, at the end of Thomas's three year contract, could not afford to pay him. Instead the man gave Thomas a set of law books. Thomas soon opened his own trading post and was very successful. Shortly thereafter he opened several more stores.

When agitation for Cherokee removal developed around 1828, several Cherokees who had taken "reservations" under the terms of an earlier treaty were afraid the federal government might not honor their treaty rights and remove them to lands farther west. They went to Thomas and requested that he represent them as their attorney. He did so and over the next several years was able to secure their rights to remain in North Carolina. He also collected the money owed to them for their share of what the government paid the Cherokees on their original eastern homelands. Thomas then used the Cherokees' money to buy land for them, as Indians were not allowed to own land in North Carolina at that time. In fact, the land he purchased became the start of what is today the Eastern Band of Cherokee Indians' reservation in North Carolina.

Thomas ran for a position on the North Carolina state senate in 1848; he won and was reelected every two years until the beginning of the Civil War, at which time he resigned his senate seat to raise a legion for the Confederate States, known as the Thomas Legion of Cherokees and Mountaineers. The legion did well during the war, and Thomas rose to the rank of colonel.

After the war, Thomas intended to resume the life he had led before the war, but his mental condition had begun to deteriorate. William Holland Thomas spent the rest of his life in and out of mental institutions. He died in 1893 and left a legacy in western North Carolina that is unmatched by anyone else.

This novel is based largely on the following sources: Mattie Russell and E. Stanley Godbold, *Confederate Colonel and Cherokee Chief*; Paul A. Thomsen, *Rebel Chief: The Motley Life of Colonel William Holland Thomas*; the Thomas Papers in the Hunter Library at Western Carolina University at Cullowhee, North Carolina; and the Thomas Papers in the Archives at the Museum of the Cherokee Indian at Cherokee, North Carolina. I am very grateful to George Frizzell at the Hunter Library and to Barbara Duncan and Ken Blankenship at the Cherokee Museum for their help.

Wil Usdi

CHAPTER ONE

Reflection

Little Will sat in his lonely cell (he called it a cell) in the state mental hospital at Morganton, North Carolina. He tended to think of himself as Little Will, or Wil Usdi, rather than as Colonel William Holland Thomas. His thoughts were clearer on things of his youth than of yesterday or last week. And even when he could recall more recent things, they were not as pleasant as things of long ago. He was getting close to ninety years old, and he had many things in his mind—when he could recall them. He liked to think of fishing in the mountains outside of his home on Raccoon Creek when he was about ten years old. He had no more pleasant memories than those. The log house he grew up in with his mother was about two miles east of Mount Prospect in North Carolina. It was surrounded by trees of all kinds, surrounded and shrouded. His whole world was green. He lived there alone with his mother, for he had never known a father. His father, whose name was Richard, had drowned in an accident some time before he was born.

He puffed up as he recalled some things he had been told about his family. His mother had made sure that he knew these things. Family was important. She was a grandniece of Lord Baltimore and was of the family of Calverts, who had been the founders of the colony of Maryland. And on his father's side, Wil was related to President Zachary Taylor and was a cousin of the great Jefferson Davis. He could remember those things and he remembered them with pride. His mother had taught him school at home, since the school was too far from their home for him to get there on time.

He also liked to hunt, and recalled hunting mostly for rabbits and squirrels, although he did remember shooting a large wild turkey one time. He grinned a wide grin when he recalled it. It was a big, beautiful bird with a large fantail, and he remembered his mother's face when he brought it home. Ah, it had made a fine meal for the two of them. Just the two of them. He could recall the succulent taste as if he had just taken a big bite. His mother had been a fine cook.

He loved the memory of those days. He had a deep fondness for the old log house and for its setting in the mountains, along the side of Raccoon Creek. But those happy days had come to an end when he was twelve years old. His mother had decided that it was time Will found his own way in the world. Life was hard for her at forty-two years of age, and Will was old enough to work at a man's job. He was well educated, she thought, even if she herself had been his teacher. So Temperance Calvert Thomas contacted her old family friend, congressman Felix Walker.

Walker was well-known, and his son had one trading post in Mount Prospect and another on Soco Creek in the Cherokee country, about thirty miles distant. He could not properly run both of the stores. He needed some help. Young Will was bright and could cipher well. He was mature for his age—although he did not look it because of his diminutive stature. Walker and his son came by the log house to visit with Will and his mother, and he brought a contract for Will to sign. The contract said that Will would be a clerk in the store and would perform all duties connected to that position. He would have one assistant, a young Cherokee boy who was already employed there. Will's time of service under the contract, which was renewable, was three years, and for that time he would receive one hundred dollars, his board, and clothing.

One hundred dollars seemed a fortune to Will at that time. He was glad to sign the contract. He was anxious to be a man and be earning his own way. When Walker was gone, Will's mother helped him to pack his clothes. There weren't very many. She also packed a few books for him. He was a voracious reader. She fixed him a fine meal of fish he had caught in Raccoon Creek the day before, corn bread, and greens, and then sent him on his way. He rode the distance from Raccoon Creek to the store on Soco Creek in a buggy with the younger Walker, and when he got to the store, he showed the contract with Walker's signature and his own on it to the Cherokee boy who was running things. Walker introduced the two boys to each other and told the Cherokee boy that Will was to be in charge of the operations of the store. Will recalled all of these things as if they had happened the day before.

The Cherokee boy was about Will's age, and he could speak English passably but not well. He was called John, but, of course, that was not his real name. His real name was Oowalookie Loony, but he did not want to be called Loony in English, and Oowalookie was too difficult for English speakers. Someone had started calling him John, and he decided that John was as good as anything else. So he was John. Will had soon decided that it would be easier to learn to speak Cherokee than to teach John better English, so he began studying. He studied by listening carefully to John when he spoke Cherokee and listening to other Cherokees speak. That was easy for he was surrounded most of the time by Cherokees.

He started by greeting Cherokees in their own language and

asking, "How are you?" Then he would ask them what he could do for them, and when he could no longer keep up the conversation in Cherokee, he would call on John for help. As time went by, he called on John less and less. He soon found that it was a great pleasure to speak in Cherokee to his customers and to carry on conversations in Cherokee with John when they were alone in the store. It wasn't long before he no longer needed to call on John for help. He could talk with anyone about anything in Cherokee for as long as he wanted. He became comfortable in the new language.

As he talked with John when they were alone, he asked John about Cherokee life. He began to learn about the things that the Cherokees ate and about their beliefs and ceremonies. John told him the old Cherokee stories. He particularly loved the old story about Brass, the Gambler, the one who had invented the game the Cherokees called *gatayusti*. He was disappointed to learn that they no longer played it. They still engaged in the rough game of *Anetsodi*, known in English as stickball; and they played marbles, not the way white boys played it, but in a particularly Cherokee way. Will wanted to learn to play Cherokee marbles and stickball and he told John so.

Of course, Will was learning other things as well. He was learning the value of pelts, and he was learning how to keep the books when he gave a Cherokee credit. And he found that he was giving a great deal of credit. Mostly the Cherokees had little money, so his bookkeeping became a very important skill. He would record the name of the Cherokee customer, perhaps, say, Bear Meat, and then he would write down what the customer had wanted, perhaps five pounds of sugar, five pounds of coffee, maybe a knife, and he would record the value of each item. He would then explain to the Indian what he had written and have the Indian sign the book, usually with a mark. Sometimes the Indian would write his own name in English letters, but that was extremely rare.

One day a big and handsome Cherokee strode into the store. "'Siyo," said Will. "What can I do for you?" But of course he continued speaking Cherokee, and the conversation continued in that language.

The big man said, "Yonaguska dagwado. 'Gado dejadoa?"

"Will dagwadoa," Will answered. "Dohiju?"

"I am just fine," answered Bear Drowning Him, for that was the name he had been given. "And how about you, Little Will?"

"I, too, am just fine," said Will. "Did you come in to buy something?"

"I just came in to see who was here. I like to know everyone around here."

"Oh. Well, I am very glad to know you, Yonaguska. Sit down and let's have a talk."

He pulled a chair out from behind the counter for Yonaguska to sit on. Drowning Bear sat down. "Is it all right if I smoke?" he asked.

"Of course," said Will.

"Do you have a pipe?"

"No," said Will. "I do not."

"Who are your parents, Wil Usdi?"

"My mother is Temperance Calvert," Will said. "My father died before I was born. I never knew him, but his name was Richard Thomas."

"And where does your mother live?"

"She lives alone on Raccoon Creek near Mount Prospect."

"That's too bad about your parents."

They continued to make small talk for several minutes before

Yonaguska got up to leave, apparently satisfied that he now knew who was running the store. Will felt satisfied that he had made a new friend and that he had carried on a conversation with the man in the Cherokee language. He had liked Yonaguska. He hoped that he would come back to visit again.

John, who had been out on an errand, came back into the store, and Will said, "John, I have just met a very interesting man. His name is Yonaguska, and we had a good talk."

"Will," said John, "you have made an important friend. Yonaguska is highly respected around here."

"Oh? He called me Little Will."

It was four days later when Will was just finishing up with a customer who was getting some goods on credit, when Yonaguska came back into the store. "'Siyo, Wil Usdi," he almost shouted out. He had a big smile on his face. "Are you well today?"

"'Siyo, Yonaguska. Yes. I'm well. And you?"

"I'm bully fine," said Yonaguska in English. Then back in Cherokee, "Where is my chair?"

Will turned to John. "John," he said, "can you finish this for me?"

John took over the deal Will had been working on, and Will fetched the chair for Yonaguska. He pulled one out for himself and sat down beside the man. Yonaguska reached into the bandoleer bag he wore over his shoulder and pulled out a pipe, which he held out to Will. "Now you have a pipe," he said. "Let's smoke." He took out his own pipe and a pouch of tobacco from which he filled both pipe bowls. Will went to the stove for an ember and lit the pipes. He was careful, for he had never smoked before, and he was afraid that he might cough or choke, but he did not. He managed it well enough. John finished with the customer and looked on in slight amazement, and a little jealousy, at the way in which Will and Yonaguska were getting along.

"Wil Usdi," said Yonaguska, "since you have no father, I'm going to make you my son. I'll be your father now."

Wil smiled comfortably as he recalled those early days. The adoption by Yonaguska had made a big difference in his life. The news spread quickly. Within a few days it seemed that just about all Cherokees knew that Yonaguska was now the father of Wil Usdi. And things started happening for Wil too. He was invited to take part in a stickball game by John, who said that the invitation had really come from the captain of the team. Wil showed up to play the way all of the players did. He wore a pair of shorts and nothing else. He and the other players were taken to the water, down at the river's edge, and there the medicine man scratched them with a turkey's claw down their backs and down the back sides of their legs—to make them run fast.

The two teams lined up facing one another on a large flat field with goals set up at either end. The goals were willow poles stuck into the ground, and the ball had to be thrown or carried between them. The two teams yelled out at one another as they moved closer together. At last a driver, the game's only official, took the ball, small enough to close one's fist around, and tossed it into the air.

From the moment the ball was first thrown, there seemed to be no rest. It was a fast-moving game. Wil tried his best to catch the ball with his ballsticks as required, but it was extremely difficult to do. He missed one ball and it came crashing down on his forehead. Then he was run over by several players who were after the ball. Wil scrambled with them all, and he actually got the ball. When he stood up to run with it, three big players from the other team tackled him and knocked the ball loose. When it was at last all over, Wil felt fortunate indeed that nothing on him was broken. He had a few scratches and bruises, but nothing worse. He felt great, though, for having played in the game.

Yonaguska came to him to go hunting also, and when he could take off from his duties at the store, Wil went with the old man. However, he soon discovered that once they were out in the woods, Yonaguska drank whiskey and would get drunk. When he did, Wil always tried to get his rifle away from him and carry it. Usually Yonaguska offered no resistance. He walked along happily with his jug, content to let Wil fire at any game that appeared. When Wil shot his first deer, he was very puffed up, and he gave the deer to Yonaguska. When they got back to the town, Yonaguska told everyone they met, with great pride, that his son, Wil Usdi, had shot the deer and made a present of it to him.

Yonaguska saw to it that Wil began dressing like a Cherokee, and very soon, for all practical purposes, Wil had become a Cherokee. He began playing Cherokee marbles, and he continued playing stickball. He even developed some proficiency with his ballsticks, both catching and throwing the ball with them. He took part in the Green Corn Dance when the time came, and he learned to sing the songs and to dance. Sometimes John was with Wil at these activities, but more often than not, one of them had to be at the store.

There was a sudden knock at the cell door, and it brought Wil back to reality and out of his reverie. "What?" he shouted. "Who is it? What do you want?"

"It's George, Mr. Thomas," came a voice through the door. "I have your supper."

"Well, come on in with it. Don't stand out there letting it get cold."

George opened the door and stepped in. He put a tray on the table. Wil noticed that, as usual, there was nothing for him to eat with except a spoon. "You're still afraid that I'll try to kill you with a fork or with a table knife, are you? Ha ha. I might. Bring me one sometime and we'll find out."

"You'll manage all right with what you have there," said George. "This looks like a good meal. I wish I had one like it right now."

"Well, get you one. What's wrong with you? Get one and eat it."

"It's not my meal time yet," said George. "I have to see that all of you are fed first."

"All of us nuts?"

"Now I didn't say that."

"No, but you thought it, didn't you? We are all nuts. Crazy as bed bugs."

"Mr. Thomas, you'd better eat your food and drink your coffee before it gets cold."

"I suppose so," said Wil, picking up his spoon.

"Oh," said George, "I nearly forgot. I have a letter here for you."

He reached inside his shirt and produced a letter, which he handed to Wil. Wil took it and looked at it. He read the return address. It was from a James Mooney in Washington, D.C. He tossed it aside. "Aren't you going to read it?" said George.

"I don't know him," said Wil, "and besides, I'll read it when you're gone. Whatever it is, it's none of your business."

"Well, all right. Hell. I'm gone," said George. "I hope you choke." He left the room, shutting the door behind him. Wil took a bite of green peas with his spoon, looked at the closed door, and reached for the letter. He ripped it open quickly, took out the letter and unfolded it. He read through it and discovered that Mooney was an ethnologist with the Bureau of American Ethnology. He said that he was assigned to write about the Cherokees, and he intended to visit the home of the Eastern Band of Cherokee Indians. He would need to interview some of them, and he would very much appreciate Wil's help in getting the names of people who would be good for him to talk with. He said he would also like to interview Wil for his knowledge of Cherokee history and culture.

Wil tossed the letter aside once more and went back to eating his meal. It wasn't too bad. It was much like everything else they gave him to eat in this madhouse. It hadn't much taste. The peas and mashed potatoes tasted much alike, as did the bread and the meat. As to what kind of meat it was, he could not say. He ate it, though, and then he went to his desk drawer for a pen and ink and some paper. He had to answer Mr. Mooney's letter.

CHAPTER TWO

The Ethnologist

There was a knock at Wil Usdi's door, and Wil jumped at the sound. Then he composed himself. "Who is it?" he shouted. The door opened and the young man in the white suit stepped inside.

"Mr. Thomas," he said, "you have a visitor."

"Who is it?"

The young man looked at a note he held in his hand. "It's a Mr. James Mooney," he said. "From Washington."

Wil brightened up some. He had gotten a letter from Mr. Mooney a few days before, and he was expecting the man. "Well, send him in," he said. "Immediately."

The young man stepped aside, and in a moment, the other stepped in. "Colonel Thomas?" he said.

Wil stood up and nodded. "Yes, indeed," he said. "I'm William Holland Thomas, known to the Cherokees as Wil Usdi." He held out his hand. Mooney took it in his and gave it a hearty shake. "I'm James Mooney," he said, "of the Bureau of American Ethnology in Washington."

"Yes, I've been expecting you. So Nimrod Smith recommended me to you."

"That's correct, Colonel Thomas," said Mooney. "I met the chief in Washington. I've been engaged by the Bureau to undertake a major study of the Cherokees, and I mean to begin in

Qualla Town. Chief Smith suggested that the best place for me to begin would be with you."

"That was very generous of Nimrod," said Wil. "What would you like to know?"

Mooney took a notebook out of his pocket and a pencil from another.

"Oh, pardon me," said Wil. "Please sit down."

"Thank you." Mooney took a chair. He put the notebook on his knee. "I would like to know who you would recommend to me as informants. What old people out on the reservation would have a treasure trove of knowledge about the old days? And would be willing to talk to me?"

"The most important would be old Ayunini, or Swimmer," said Wil. "He's a veritable storehouse of valuable information. During the late war, he was a second sergeant in Company A of my legion. You must meet and visit with Swimmer."

Mooney wrote the name in his notebook. Wil noted with satisfaction that Mooney was not a big man, only a few inches taller than himself. He was a dapper dresser, wearing a three-piece suit and sporting a fine mustache. And he was a very young man, probably less than thirty years old. "What can you tell me of the game of stickball?" Mooney asked.

"We call it *Anetsodi* in Cherokee," said Wil. "It's the Little Brother of War. It's played on a large field with a goal at each end. The object is to get the ball through the goals. There are two branches stuck in the ground for each goal. The ball is small. You can close your fist around it. It's made of animal skins. Each player carries two ballsticks. Each stick is about a yard long with a small racquet or web at the end. A skilled ballplayer can catch the ball in flight between the two webbed racquets at the end of his sticks, and he can throw it with them as well. There are no boundaries, so if a crowd is watching the game and the ball goes in their direction, they had better scatter, for the game will be coming toward them. In the old days, it was not uncommon for a player to be killed occasionally, but nowadays the games are not so rough. The worst anyone may expect today is a broken bone or a bloody nose."

Mooney was busy writing this all down in his notebook. When Wil finished his report, he went to the door and called out. One of the attendants showed up quickly, and Wil demanded that two cups of coffee be brought to his room. The man fetched them right away. Wil noted to himself that he would never get such fast and polite attention if he were alone in his cell. The man was reacting to the fact that Wil had a distinguished visitor with him.

Mooney asked further questions and Wil answered them all. When Mooney asked about old stories, Wil said he could repeat one that he knew, and then he asked rather unexpectedly, "Is it going to rain?"

"No," said Mooney. "I don't think so."

"On the southern slope of the ridge, along the trail from Robbinsville to Valley River, in Cherokee County, North Carolina, are the remains of a number of stone cairns," said Wil. "The piles are leveled now, but thirty years ago, the stones were still heaped up into pyramids, to which every Cherokee who passed added a stone. According to the tradition, these piles mark the graves of a number of women and children of the tribe who were surprised and killed on the spot by a raiding party of the Iroquois shortly before the final peace between the two Nations. As soon as the news was brought to the settlements on Hiwassee and Cheowa, a party was made under *Tale tanigi ski*, Hemp Carrier, to follow and take vengeance on the enemy. Among others of the party was the father of the noted chief *Tsunu lahun ski*, or Junaluska, who died on Cheowa about 1855.

"For days they followed the trail of the Iroquois across the Great Smoky mountains, through forests and over rivers, until they finally tracked them to their very town in the far northern Seneca country. On the way they met another war party headed for the south, and the Cherokees killed them all and took their scalps. When they came near the Seneca town, it was almost night, and they heard shouts in the townhouse, where the women were dancing over the fresh Cherokee scalps. The avengers hid themselves near the spring, and as the dancers came down to drink, the Cherokees silently killed one and then another and another, until they had counted as many scalps as had been taken on Cheowa; and still the dancers in the townhouse never thought that their enemies were near. Then, the Cherokee leader said, 'We have covered the scalps of our women and children. Shall we go home now like cowards, or shall we raise the war whoop and let the Seneca know that we are men?' 'Let them come, if they will,' said his men; and they raised the scalp yell of the Cherokee. At once there was an answering shout from within the townhouse, and the dance came to a sudden stop. The Seneca warriors swarmed out with ready guns and hatchets, but the nimble Cherokee were off and away. There was a hot pursuit in the darkness, but the Cherokee knew the trails and were light and active runners. They managed to get away with the loss of only a single man. The rest got home safely, and the people were so well pleased with Hemp Carrier's bravery and success that they gave him seven wives."

Mooney jotted this tale down in accurate detail. He marveled at the seeming sanity and command of wits that Colonel Thomas displayed, and the way the man had such control of all his faculties. He had been warned that Colonel Thomas was a madman—although he did have occasional lucid moments. Mooney had come prepared for almost anything that might happen. But Colonel Thomas behaved as an almost perfect gentleman and appeared, furthermore, to be a very bright one. Mooney was much pleased at the success of his first visit with Colonel Thomas, and he sincerely hoped that there would be more.

"When you visit with Swimmer," said Wil, "you will get many more stories, much better even than this one I have just told you."

Wil and Mooney had a long visit, but now and then Wil would appear to be distracted and would say something that had nothing to do with their conversation. Then he would come back to the point. At last Mooney excused himself and took his leave. For a time Wil sat glorying in his reputation and feeling in high spirits for having been interviewed by a distinguished visitor from the Bureau of American Ethnology. And the man was actually impressed by him! He could tell. But before long his mind began to wander, and it went back to Raccoon Creek and the rabbit and squirrel hunting adventures he had there. He thought about his mother. He wondered about his father.

Then he asked himself, "How old am I?" He could not recall. It seemed an important question to him. One should know his own age. He had no idea. Was he thirty-five? Sixty? Seventy? He wasn't at all sure. Where was his wife? Where were his children? Why was he in this cell and not in one of his seven stores? Where was old Yonaguska? Were the Yankees coming? How could he keep his Cherokees from being moved to the West? Had John Cockerham delivered the 1,000 rails yet to Stekoih? He knew that he had written a letter to Thomas Armstrong regarding John Tatham's claim for his hogs that had been killed by soldiers, but he had not yet received an answer from Armstrong. What was wrong with Armstrong?

He thought about the delicious barbecued deer the Indians had prepared on top of Soco Mountain, and he wondered when they would do that again. He would certainly be delighted to have such a sumptuous feast again, and he hoped that it would not be too long coming. What day of the week was it? Come Sunday he would have to go to his mother's house again. He did not like putting off visits to his mother for too long. He suddenly had a roaring in his ear, and he banged the side of his head with his right hand.

"Damn it," he said.

There was another knock on his cell door, and he shouted, "Who is it? What do you want?"

The door opened, and the white-suited attendant stepped in. "Mr. Thomas," the young man said, "supper's ready. Will you come out?"

"Have I had a letter from President Johnson yet?" demanded Wil.

"Not yet," said the youth, with a smug look on his face. He was thinking, Johnson is not even the president any more, you old fool, but to his credit, he kept that remark to himself.

"How old am I?" Wil asked the young man.

"You don't know?"

"Would I ask you if I knew? How old am I?"

"Well, I believe you are eighty-seven years old. Maybe eighty-eight now. I'm not sure."

"Eighty-eight," said Wil. "How could I be that old?"

"You just lived that long is all. Are you going to come out to supper?"

"No."

"I'll have something brought in for you then." He turned and stepped out of the room, shutting the door behind himself.

"Eighty-what?" said Wil to himself. "How damn old am I?"

He stood up and walked across the room. Then he turned and headed back toward the chair he had been sitting in. On the way, he stumbled over the rug in the center of the room and nearly fell, but then managed to catch his balance. He thought, how lucky I am. I could have broken a bone. He got back to the chair and sat down heavily.

"How old am I?" he said.

Someone came in bringing a tray.

"Did you bring my chicken soup?" said Wil.

"I brought your meal. There's no chicken soup, though."

Wil looked at the fare when the tray was placed on the table—with one spoon. "No fork?" he said. "Why can't I have a fork? Bring me a fork and I'll stab you with it."

"That's why you can't have a fork—or a knife for that matter. Use what you've got and eat your meal."

There was a piece of meat on the plate. Was it beef, pork? He couldn't be sure, but he waited until the person had left the room before he picked up the spoon and started trying to slice out a bite with it. He finally tore off a corner of the nondescript meat and shoved it in his mouth. He chewed. It had no taste. He still did not know what it was. He swallowed it down and made a disgusted noise.

There were some beans on the plate and he took a spoonful of those and chewed them. They tasted to him just like the meat.

"What's wrong with the cooks in this place?" he said. "They're awful. I don't know what they are, but they're not cooks. They may be chicken pluckers for all I know. Goddamned tasteless stuff. It's not really even food. I'll starve to death in this place. How damn old am I anyway?"

CHAPTER THREE

The Young Entrepreneur

Wil lay in his bed trying to sleep, but sleep was elusive. It would not come. He was recalling his youth, after he had worked for the son of Felix Walker, the congressman, for three years as a clerk in his trading post on Soco Creek. It was time for him to be paid, and he was anxious to receive the $100 that had been promised him by contract. He was anxious for Walker to show up at the store. When Walker finally did come, it was late in the day, and he was wearing a long face and carrying a rather large box in his arms.

Wil was dressed like a Cherokee in clothes that Yonaguska had chosen for him to wear. He wore moccasins and leggings, and on top he had on a trade shirt and over all a beautiful hunting jacket. "'Siyo, Mr. Walker," he said. "How are you, sir?" Walker strode over to the counter and put the box, which seemed to be heavy, onto the counter. "Hello, William," he said. "I'm afraid I have come with bad news."

Wil's expression changed to a more compassionate one. "What news, sir?" he said.

"I have been forced into bankruptcy, William. I'm closing my stores. What's worse, for you, I cannot afford to pay you the money I owe you. I've brought these books for you in lieu of pay-ment." He reached into the box and pulled out, one at a time, a set of law books. "If you will study these, they'll pay you back ten times over, more than the $100 would have been worth to you."

At first Wil's expression betrayed a deep disappointment, but then he picked up one of the books and flipped through some of the pages. It looked to him to be fascinating, and even at the young age of fifteen, he thought he could see a bright future ahead for himself—if he would only take full advantage of these books. "Thank you, sir," he said. "I will study them diligently."

"I wish you good use of them," said Walker.

Wil, now out of a job, spent long hours at his mother's house studying the law books. He almost memorized them. If any question regarding the law came up that he could not answer immediately, he could pick up one of the books and find the answer at once. He divided his time between the community at Soco Creek and his mother's house. His mother was saddened that the job for Walker had not worked out, but she was pleased about Wil's progress with the law books.

"It was not young Mr. Walker's fault," she said, "that his business failed. He just had too much to do and couldn't keep up with everything."

But, Wil thought, it was not my fault either. I did a good job with his store. Whoever was running his other store may have been to blame, but not me. Certainly not me. He told his mother how he had learned the business so well that he knew he could run a profitable store. At last she decided that he was right. She sold a few acres of her property and gave Wil the money he would need to open his own place of business.

Wil opened his store out at Soco Creek, right where the Walker store had been, and he did extremely well with it. The Cherokees already knew him and trusted him. They liked it that he spoke Cherokee with them. Sometimes they paid him money and sometimes they paid him in skins or hogs or even in bushels of corn. He very meticulously calculated the value of each item they brought him for payment, and he kept careful records of all his transactions. Yonaguska, like a real father, kept close tabs on Wil, and Wil still dressed like a Cherokee.

Life was good for Wil when he was fifteen, sixteen, and seventeen years old. He was making money; in fact, he was becoming a wealthy young man. He gave much of his money to his mother, in part to pay her back for having financed his operation. He still played stickball with his Cherokee friends, and he attended the dances and ceremonies. But then this idyllic life was threatened. The state of Georgia began agitating the U.S. government to get the Cherokees out of their territory. In 1802, the state had signed an agreement with the federal government in which the government had agreed to remove the Cherokees as soon as it was convenient. The other states in which the Cherokees lived, Alabama, South Carolina, and Tennessee, now also joined in the fray. They all wanted the Cherokees out. A heated national debate ensued.

By 1824, Wil had opened two more stores, one on Scott's Creek and one in Murphy, North Carolina. All three stores were doing good business. He was thinking of opening more. But the Cherokee Nation was in turmoil. However, in 1819, a number of Cherokees had affixed their names to a treaty with the United States, in which they had purchased a huge tract of Cherokee land. In this treaty, the Cherokees requested and were granted "reservations" for themselves—as individual citizens of North Carolina—where they could "reside permanently." They remained somewhat separated from the turmoil. Yonaguska was one of these, and he settled near the junction of Soco Creek and the Oconaluftee River.

The new Principal Chief of the Cherokee Nation, John Ross, was doing everything he could to keep the Cherokees in their homeland. He had some prominent Cherokees as his allies in this fight: Major Ridge, his son John, Elias Boudinot, and others. These men were running around the eastern part of the United States giving lectures on the subject, and soon the Cherokee Nation began to publish a newspaper with Elias Boudinot as its editor. Just a few years earlier a Cherokee named Sequoyah had presented the Cherokees with a syllabary, a sort of alphabet by which they could read and write in their own language. The Cherokee Nation's newspaper was published in a bilingual edition. Wil taught himself to use the syllabary and delighted in reading the Cherokee language version first.

Yonaguska and others came to see Wil one day in his store. Wil and Yonaguska gathered some chairs and set them around so that everyone could have a seat. "Wil Usdi," said Yonaguska, "all of these people with me and I have our little reservations. We applied for them with a treaty a few years ago, and the government gave them to us. They said that we are no longer a part of the Cherokee Nation, and they said that we can live on them for good as citizens of the state of North Carolina."

"Yes," said Wil, "I remember that."

"Now they're talking about making the Cherokee Nation move some place out West. Will we be safe on our reservations?"

"You certainly should be," said Wil. "They're talking about moving the Cherokee Nation, and you are no longer a part of that Nation."

"But sometimes I hear it said that all Cherokees will be forced to move. Does that mean us? We are still Cherokees."

"I believe that you'll be safe."

"You studied all those law books," said Yonaguska. "I want you to be sure. We all have talked about this. If the last Cherokee gets kicked out of these mountains, there will be no more Cherokees.

Wil Usdi, we can't let that happen. There must be Cherokees. We can't let them destroy us."

"I'll look into it, Father," said Wil. "They won't destroy you."

"Good," said Yonaguska. "I want you to be our lawyer."

Soon thereafter, the case was taken up in the North Carolina Supreme Court, and the court upheld the treaty and the rights of the Cherokees who had signed the treaties to remain on their land. Yonaguska's faith in Wil Usdi was also upheld. The boy had become a man at nineteen years of age. He could be relied on. Yonaguska was proud of his adopted son, and he was proud that no matter what happened, there would always be Cherokees in the mountains of North Carolina.

Most of the Cherokees who had won the court case lived near Yonaguska, along Soco Creek or the banks of the Oconaluftee River. People began calling them the Luftee Indians, and these Luftee Indians began looking at Yonaguska as their main advisor, almost as their chief. They no longer saw themselves as a part of the Cherokee Nation.

Around that time, Georgia became extremely aggressive and passed a series of anti-Cherokee laws calculated to make life so miserable for the Cherokees that they would be anxious to leave. Happily for Wil Usdi and the Luftees in North Carolina, they were well away from all that. In spite of that fact, Wil Usdi knew what was happening in Georgia, and years later, in his late eighties and sitting in his cell at the madhouse, he recalled the details vividly.

By 1831, Wil owned seven stores and he was acknowledged by all of the Luftee Indians as their attorney. At twenty-six, he was a very wealthy man. Now it was astonishing, even to Wil himself, that an old man who could not even remember his age could recall all of this in such detail.

The Cherokee Nation under the leadership of Chief John Ross continued to fight the good fight, and in 1832, Reverend Samuel Worcester, a missionary who had been arrested in Georgia for residing on Cherokee lands without a permit from the state of Georgia, took his case to the U.S. Supreme Court. The court ruled in his favor and in favor of the Cherokee Nation, saying that states' rights must give way to federal rights in cases involving Indian tribes. The Cherokee Nation celebrated for a time, until they heard that President Andrew Jackson had said something like, "John Marshall has made his decision; now let him enforce it." In other words, the federal government was going to look the other way and let Georgia do as it wanted to do, ignoring federal laws.

At that point, the Ridges and Elias Boudinot and their followers decided that the Cherokee Nation had gone as far as it could go, and that the best recourse for the Cherokees at that point would be to give in and agree to move West. They got together with government negotiators and signed the 1835 Treaty of New Echota, a treaty of total removal. Still, John Ross urged the Cherokees to stay put, and they did. Those who signed the treaty, none of them Cherokee Nation officials, became known as the Treaty Party, and they moved right away. The rest of the Cherokees, the majority Ross Party, continued to resist.

In 1838, the U.S. Army was sent to round up the Cherokees and forcibly move them West. It was a miserable business, and Wil Usdi was fully aware of it. North Carolina was still home to 3,644 Cherokees, and the federal government was obligated to round them up—all of them except the Luftee Indians. When they began the roundup, they met with serious resistance, particularly from one source.

A Cherokee named Tsali and his family were captured and

being marched to one of the stockades where Cherokees were held prior to their removal. Along the way, a soldier mistreated Tsali's wife, and Tsali killed the soldier. He then immediately fled with his family into the mountains. But the Army wanted justice. General Scott, who was in charge of the removal, said that he would leave off the hunt for more Cherokees if Tsali and his accomplices would surrender. General Scott managed to get hold of Wil Usdi, and Wil said that he thought he could find Tsali.

Wil Usdi went to Euchella, a Luftee who headed a band of refugees in the mountains. Euchella agreed to go with him to find Tsali. When they found Tsali, who was living in the mountains with his family, they told him what General Scott had said. Tsali thought it all over. Finally, he said, "I do not want my own people to hunt me down, and I do want the Army to leave everyone else alone. I'll go down with you."

As they went down the mountain, toward where Wil knew that Tsali would be executed, Wil grieved for Tsali. This was a selfless thing he was doing. He was giving his own life so that others would be able to stay in these mountains, the mountains that they all loved so much, loved with everything they had, so that Cherokees would remain in the mountains, and so there would always be Cherokees. It was not an easy thing to say: All right, for the good of all, I will give myself to be shot. Tsali was saving the people, or he was saving the homes of his people. Anyway you chose to express it, it was a brave and generous act.

Wil had not known what to expect from Tsali. He did not know Tsali well. He had only hoped that his arguments and those of Euchella would work on the man. And if Tsali were a follower of Chief John Ross, then he would know that Ross had told the people not to fight. Ross was still pursuing legal routes, and Ross knew that another war with the United States would prove to be fruitless.

A brief trial was held when they got back to the Army's headquarters, and Tsali and his oldest sons were condemned. They were stood against trees. A firing squad was made up of some of Euchella's band of Cherokees. Tsali stood straight and tall, and the squad fired. The bodies were given to Tsali's wife for burial.

Contemplating this old story alone in his room, or cell, Wil wept. Whenever he took the time to ponder on those events, he wept. The whole miserable event now known as the Trail of Tears caused him much grief. Many of his old friends had gone West on that terrible trek. A number of them had died along the way. And what had it all been for? From the point of view of the U.S. government, it had been for Manifest Destiny. It had to happen, for the Cherokees were in the way. Progress took precedent over all. Sometimes Wil hated the U.S. government. Sometimes he wished that Chief Ross had not told the Cherokees to remain peaceful.

A war would have been good, even if the Cherokees had lost. They could have killed a good many whites and at least felt a little better about it. But they had not fought, and things were what they were. It had all been a long time ago.

And what of those fortunate few, the ones who remained behind? How had it been for them? About fourteen hundred Cherokees remained in the East; seven hundred in and around Quallatown, the name they had given to the settlement on the Oconaluftee; four hundred or so scattered along the Cheoah, Valley, and Hiwassee rivers; and even fewer still in Georgia, Tennessee, and Alabama. The country seemed very lonely for a Cherokee then—even for a white man who believed himself to be Cherokee. It had largely been emptied of Cherokee people. It was not empty, though, for white people were moving in where the Cherokees had been. Wil recalled some of the many times he had ridden up to a lone cabin in the mountains where Cherokees had once lived, only to see a white farmer; and he remembered how disappointing that feeling had been.

How he longed for the old days, the days when Cherokees were everywhere, when almost all of his neighbors had been Cherokee, when he dressed like a Cherokee and spoke the Cherokee language to everyone he met and played ball with them, went hunting with them, and generally lived his life with them.

During the removal and after it, old Yonaguska had become a confirmed drunk. That always made Wil sad. He didn't like seeing the old man thus. But then one day, Yonaguska had simply fallen down dead, it seemed. They had laid him out in his bed and were preparing for his burial, when he suddenly sat up again and opened his eyes. "I've been talking with God!" he said. Everyone around had been astounded. Wil had not been present, but someone had been sent running for him right away; and when Wil heard the word, he ran all the way back to Yonaguska's house, leaving his store unattended. When Wil stepped into the room, old Yonaguska had smiled a broad smile. "Ah, my son," he said, "it's good that you've come. I died, you know, but now I've come back. I had a long talk with God. He told me that I've been doing wrong things. Cherokees should not drink the white man's wisgi. He told me to stop it, and to tell all Cherokees to leave it alone. So I say now that I will never drink wisgi again. Never. The other thing he told me to say to the People was that they should never leave this land. Never."

With Wil's help, Yonaguska organized a Cherokee Temperance Society. He kept his word and never drank spirits again, and what's more, most all of the Cherokees joined his Society and left off drinking booze. Wil's time was divided between the activities of Yonaguska's Temperance Society, his own stores, and visiting his mother. Finally, in 1839, Yonaguska died a second time. Lying on his death bed, he said to those gathered around him, "Never leave these mountains. This is your home. If you leave these mountains, there will be no more Cherokees on the face of this earth. Stay. Stay in these mountains."

Wil missed Yonaguska terribly after the old man died. He longed for his conversation, his companionship, his guidance. But he now had to rely on himself, and he knew the Cherokees had to rely on him as well. He made a trip to Washington to plead for the Luftee Indians' share of the money the government was paying for all of the Cherokee land east of the Mississippi. He was suddenly more grateful than ever before, that old Walker had given him the law books in lieu of his $100. He won over the Congress, and he got the money for the Cherokees; but it was given to him, to William Holland Thomas, instead of to the Cherokees. Wil went home and began buying land. It was recorded in his name, for it was against the law in North Carolina in those days for Indians to own land.

Wil bought the land along the Oconaluftee. No one seemed to care. The land was too rugged, too mountainous for whites to give a damn about. He bought other land. He bought some of it with his own money. The Cherokees were secure on his land. Wil was doing so much for the Cherokees, and they were depending so much on him that people began calling Wil the white chief of the Cherokees. Of course, he was not their chief, and he knew it better than anyone else. He was their lawyer, and he was doing all that he could do for them. But he was doing it as a legal advisor. Not as their chief.

Yonaguska had been their chief, and he had died. They had

elected no other since then. They did not seem to need one or care. With Wil's help, they divided their land on the Oconaluftee into districts, and then they named the districts, also with his help and advice. The new districts were Paint Town, Bird Town, Yellow Hill, Big Cove, and Wolf Town. Without Yonaguska's leadership, the Temperance Society floundered, and some Cherokees began to drink alcohol again. Wil did what he could, but he could not stop them. He lacked some quality that Yonaguska had possessed.

His time was now occupied by his stores and by the acquisition of land for the Cherokees. Both projects were going well. He became a major landholder in western North Carolina. Of course, most of his land was what he had bought for the Cherokees, not for himself. His stores, however, were his own and were doing well. He now had more white customers than Cherokees and was becoming a wealthy man. And he learned, slowly, that he had also become a very popular figure in the western part of the state.

In 1848, when he was forty-three years old, he decided to run for the North Carolina State Senate. He was not surprised when he won; he had expected that outcome.

CHAPTER FOUR

The State Senator

George brought him his breakfast one morning, and Wil went into a tantrum. "Get out of here," he said. "Take that away. You've been poisoning my food. I know you have. Take it away." George was frightened. Wil was being much too loud.

"Just eat your breakfast," he said. "It's not poison. I promise you."

"You lie to me as well," screamed Wil. "I'd kill you if I could find my gun. A knife even. Take that poison out of here at once."

George left the cell quickly. Wil followed him to the door and pulled it open again. He looked after George where he was scurrying down the hallway. "You're trying to kill me," he yelled. "Poison. Poison. They're poisoning my food. Trying to kill me. Damn you. Damn you all."

He slammed the door and went back to his chair. Almost immediately he began craving a cup of coffee. But would it be poisoned as well? How could he be sure? He went back to the door and opened it wide. "George," he shouted. "George."

In a couple of minutes, George was back. "Bring me some coffee," said Wil. "Bring the pot and two cups."

George left, and soon he was back with the coffee pot and two cups. Wil had him pour one cup. "Now drink it," he said. George seemed puzzled, but he drank it. Wil watched him for a moment, and when he did not drop dead, he had him pour the other cup full. He took that one for himself and sat down in his chair to enjoy it.

"You didn't get any poison in the coffee yet, did you?" he said.

George left muttering to himself, but Wil could not understand any of the mumbling. He quietly sipped his coffee. He was glad the coffee had not been poisoned. He wondered how much poison he had already consumed. Had it been enough to kill him? Of course, he could not be sure. It had not yet even made him sick. They were probably only using small amounts, hoping that it would not be detected but would kill him over a period of time.

Suddenly he thought of Catharine. She had been his first love. And how he had loved her. He had loved her in every way he could think of. Their first time had been in the back room of his store. He had locked the front door and led her to the back room. He had started by kissing her. On her luscious lips, and on her pretty white neck. He had kissed her shoulders, and soon he had her round breasts exposed. Oh, what a time that had been. He would never forget it even if he had wanted to.

Eventually she had moved into his house with him, and they'd had five children together: Wesley, Nancy Julette, William Pendelton, Eliza Ann, and Keener. Since Wil and Catharine never married, all of the children used their mother's last name of Hyde. Wil and Catharine had some good years together, but they were not to last. Nothing lasted. Nothing good lasted. The only thing that lasted was this damnable cell he was living in. No. Not living. Existing only. They were trying to bring an end to it, though, by poisoning him. "How old am I?" he suddenly asked himself.

He remembered that his first years in the senate had been good years. He had made new friends, and he began to make an impression on the rest of the state. He began to make himself known and respected around the entire state, not just the western end of it. He did not raise any hell, and so he did not make any enemies. Not that he could tell.

He continued working for the Cherokees, who by this time were known as the Eastern Band of Cherokee Indians. He acquired citizenship in the state of North Carolina for them, but they did not try to vote or to exercise any of the privileges of citizenship. He knew that he also had to do things for the white citizens of western North Carolina. He inaugurated a system of road improvements for western North Carolina, and he was instrumental in getting the Western North Carolina Railroad system in place to benefit the copper mines of Ducktown, Tennessee. He was doing good things for his part of the state, and he knew it. His constituents knew it as well, for they re-elected him in 1850.

Senator William Holland Thomas was a prominent and well-respected citizen of the state in 1850. All in all, he figured, he had done great things. He had amassed a small fortune, become an influential politician, and although it was not true, was known widely as Chief of the Eastern Band of Cherokee Indians. Not bad for a poor North Carolina mountain boy of only forty-five years.

Somewhere along the way, he had lost Catharine Hyde. Try as he might, sitting in his cell, he could not remember what had happened. She was gone. That was all. Gone where? He did not know. Why? He did not know that either. And where were his children? His Hyde children? They did not come to see him. He did not think that his whole Hyde family was dead. They were just gone was all. Out of his life.

But then he had met Elizabeth, and she had been wonderful. Sitting there thinking about her, he recalled every intimate detail of their lovemaking. It had been glorious, and it had made one son, a fine boy they named William Patrick. William Patrick Rose. He had also taken his mother's last name. Why did they all take their mother's names and not his? He did not know, and he wondered why he had no children with his own last name. What was wrong with Thomas for a name? Then he wondered for a moment if they were involved with the people at this place in a conspiracy to poison him. He dismissed that thought. He did not believe that they were such wretches.

Nothing lasts. Elizabeth Rose was gone from his life just like Catharine Hyde. Did they visit with one another? Were they both dead? Or were they alive yet and now old grandmothers with no teeth? It was hard to think of them as old. He could think of himself that way, but not these lovely young things with whom he had made passionate love. Perhaps it was best that they had left his life, for now he had only lovely memories of them, memories that would never be spoiled by the ravages of time.

He had also had a wonderful affair with a fine-looking young Cherokee girl whose Cherokee name was Kanaka. She had been known in English as Angeline. Oh, how he had loved her. He tried to recall all the details, and he tried to remember what had become of her, but his mind was weak these days. There were lots of things he could no longer call up from his past, and sometimes these days of his past were just last week. He did know that he and Kanaka had produced one darling daughter they had named Demaris Angeline. She had been a beautiful little girl. And they were both gone from him now.

He recalled dandling Demaris Angeline on his knee and what a wonderful feeling that had been. She had been a beautiful child, perhaps the most beautiful he had ever seen, and she had loved him so much, perhaps as much as he had loved her. He thought about the time when she was about three years old. She had walked up to him as he was sitting in his chair and put her hands on his knees and looked up into his face and said, "I love you." It made him cry to recall such moments in his life.

He knew that he had been re-elected to the senate again in 1852, and he had continued acquiring land and improving roads in his part of the state. His business ventures kept improving. One of the most profitable parts of his business was the buying and selling of ginseng, which Cherokees gathered for him from the forested mountainsides and he then resold for the market in China. He owed much of his wealth to *sang*. He wondered if the *sang* did all for the Chinese that they believed it to do.

When was Mooney coming back? He had so much enjoyed his visit with Mooney. And how long ago had it been? He couldn't be sure. It might have been last week, or it might have been some years ago. Oh, Mooney. How is your work going, Mooney? I wish you much luck of it.

For a moment he thought that he was about to be late for a senate session. He wondered what year it was. He went to the door and called out to George. George did not come, but another attendant did. "George is not here just now," said the white-suited attendant. "May I help you?"

"What year is it?" said Wil in desperation.

"Why, it's 1890, Colonel Thomas."

"1890," Wil repeated. "I was elected for the last time in 1860. After all, I don't have to go. How old am I?"

"I believe you're eighty-five years old," the attendant said.

"Eighty-five," said Wil. "I like you. You're not putting poison in my food. It's George and the others. Not you though."

The attendant left, and Wil went to his bed. He stretched himself out at his full length and clasped his hands behind his head. "I'm an old man," he said. "I'm—how old?"

He had been last elected to the senate in 1860. He contemplated that. That was his final term. What had happened? He recalled that he and his colleagues had voted to secede from the Union. He had been opposed to secession at first, but had at last been persuaded and then voted for it. They had been working for years, through his many terms, to establish a place they called the North Carolina Lunatic Asylum at Dix Hill in Raleigh, the state capitol. If only he had known then that they would later imprison him in the dreadful place.

Then the next thing he had done was to go back to Quallatown to talk to the Cherokees there. In no time, he had raised four hundred Cherokees for a legion. He decided that he needed more men than he could raise among the Cherokees, so he recruited whites from the surrounding areas. He created the Thomas Legion of Cherokee Indians and Highlanders. Wil, now fifty-seven years old, was elected captain of the legion. They were assigned to Tennessee.

On their way to Knoxville, they enlisted all the young Cherokee men they came across. They traveled fifty miles in two days and reached Valleytown. While they waited in Valleytown, it began to rain. Soon the Valley River was swollen, and they could not cross. They waited a few days. They knew they could not cross with their wagon, so when they decided that they could wait no longer, they took the wagon apart and carried it a piece at a time across the high footbridge that crossed the river. Wil recalled the trip to Knoxville vividly.

The next night, they camped on the Tennessee side of the line, and by noon they had reached Sweetwater, a stop along the Tennessee and Georgia Railroad. It was but a short rail trip from there to Knoxville. Wil went with Major Morgan, known to the Cherokees as Agan'stat,' on a train to Knoxville ahead of the rest to make preparations for their arrival. Morgan was a half blood, his father Gideon having fought at the Battle of Horseshoe Bend with Andrew Jackson, the Chicken Snake. The rest of the legion caught a later train.

Wil and Agan'stat' met the train when it arrived in Knoxville. They formed up the unit and marched it through town to a hill on the north side where they made camp and named it Camp Aganstata. It overlooked the city of Knoxville. The Thomas Legion made quite a stir as it marched through the city. A great many citizens of Knoxville lined the streets to observe. They found the Indians in Confederate uniforms a fascinating sight. Wil Usdi was proud of his legion at that time.

Wil suddenly got up from his chair and walked to the closet. He fumbled through the clothes hanging there until he found his old Confederate jacket. Pulling off his dressing gown, he tossed it aside and put on the jacket. He buttoned the buttons that he could and stood up straight as a pin. He looked around for his gun and his saber, but he could not find them. He really wanted them. He wanted to kill the people who were poisoning his food—trying to kill him.

He thought about the church service they had held, when many Knoxville citizens showed up to get a look at the Cherokee Confederates in their new uniforms. Unaguska, the grandson of old Yonaguska, was the chaplain of the outfit, and he delivered a rousing sermon in the Cherokee language. Wil listened intently. The Cherokees all sat proud, enjoying the attention they were getting from the crowd.

After fourteen days of drilling and hanging about the camp, the legion was ordered to Strawberry Plains, north of Knoxville, to guard its railroad bridge. First Lieutenant James Terrell, who had been employed by Wil before as his assistant, remarked to

Wil as the troops were leaving for Strawberry Plains, "Most of these men are armed but with squirrel rifles. They would be better off with bows and arrows." Wil had to agree, but he had so far been unsuccessful in getting the Confederacy to supply them with new rifles.

Wil recalled that the Cherokees named their new camp after the great Junaluska. Soon a fever struck the camp. It was followed by measles and then by mumps. The Cherokees did not even have a name for mumps. In due time, the sicknesses ran their course. It was reported that an attempt to burn the bridge was in the works, but it never materialized. Wil used his time courting General Kirby Smith and writing letters to his cousin Jefferson Davis. He was trying to get permission to raise more troops and build his Cherokee battalion into a regiment.

Wil now had two Indian companies and three other companies transferred to him. He was promoted to the rank of major. He wrote to President Davis that his Highland Rangers, as he was now calling them, was just a step in the direction of a legion. Wil badly wanted a legion, combined forces of cavalry, infantry, and artillery, all under one command—his.

James Robert Love then came into the picture. But thinking of Love sent Wil's mind to wandering again. In 1858 he had met and married James Love's daughter, Sarah Jane Love. It had been a marvelous marriage, for the Loves were one of the most prominent families in North Carolina. Marrying into that family had been a major coup for Wil. On top of that, Wil, in spite of his three earlier loves, considered Sarah to be the love of his life. He would never again need another woman. Sarah fulfilled his every wish, his every dream. She was beautiful, industrious, educated, talented, and most of all, devoted to him. Wil was at last a happily married man.

He and Sarah started a family with Margaret Elizabeth, a beautiful child who favored her mother. Their second child was a boy whom Wil named for himself: William Holland Thomas, Jr. Finally, he had children who bore his name and would carry it on for him into future generations. That was about the only thing about the war that really troubled Wil, the separation from his family that it caused.

He now had a home for that family. A house he had built on the site of old Stekoih, a town that had been destroyed by Rutherford in 1776. He was proud of his home and called it by the name of the old town, Stekoih. It was not far from the town on the Oconaluftee, which was now being called Yellow Hill, and when the house at Stekoih was finished, he moved his mother there. Wil had developed a happy home life, which the war had now disrupted. While he was away from home, at least his Sarah and his mother had each other for company.

Sitting alone in his cell, Wil thought for a moment that the war was still raging, for he was still separated from his family. What could be keeping him from them but the war? All of a sudden he hated the war and the Confederacy for the trouble they had inflicted on him and his family. He longed to see his wife, Sarah, and his children, little Margaret Elizabeth and William, Jr. And—but the war was over. So what had become of Sarah and the children? Why did they never come to visit him in his prison cell? Or if they did, why did he not remember?

"Oh, let me not be mad. Not mad, sweet heaven. Keep me in temper; I would not be mad!"

He stood up and pulled the Confederate jacket off. Then he flung it across the room. He did not want to be wearing it anymore. He detested it and all the memories it brought to him.

Wil's father-in-law, James Love, was a younger man than he.

Before the war, he had been a member of the North Carolina state legislature. But by the time he ran across Wil's path during the war, he was captain of Company A of the Sixteenth North Carolina Infantry. Love's company, along with another, was attached to Wil's, and their combined strength gave Wil the regiment he had so desired. He was promoted to colonel, and Love was elected to the office of lieutenant colonel, second in command. Wil was pleased, for in a way, this put him back in the fold of his family.

CHAPTER FIVE

Memories

Wil was at his mother's house. She had recently moved to a cabin on the Oconaluftee, not far from his first store. She was delighted to have him at home. For all that, she was thrilled to be living with him again. She had prepared a meal of fine venison that Wil had provided for them. It was good to be feeding her son at home again. And Wil ate voraciously. No matter how many good meals he had, he always felt that there was none better than what his mother fixed.

"That was delicious, Mother," he said.

"I'm glad that you enjoyed it. Will you have a little more?"

"Oh, no, Mother. I'm already stuffed to the gills. I can't eat another bite."

"Willie," she said, "I'm so proud of you. You've become an important man. You have money, and you have land. I believe that you're the biggest landowner in this part of the state."

"No. Not quite, Mother. There is that James Love. I think he has more land than I do. But I'll pass him up soon."

"And you're a senator. You've accomplished great things in your life."

"Mother," said Wil, "it's all because of the fine education you gave me, and the set of law books that I received from Mr. Walker. And even those were due to you, because you set me up with that job. I owe you all my success."

"I just did what any mother should do, Willie. It was my job to see you get a good start in life."

"And you did it very well indeed. I love you, Mother."

She leaned over and kissed him on the forehead. "And I love you, my darling boy."

Shortly after that conversation, Mr. James Love sent an invitation to Wil to attend a party he was having at his home. Wil did not know Love, and he struggled to decide whether to attend or to decline. At last he decided that he would go to the party. He dressed in his finest suit of clothes, with a vest and a tie, and he wore a new black hat with a wide, flat brim. He saddled his best horse and rode to the home of Love. He was met outside the front door by a black slave who took his horse. Another opened the front door for him, and when Wil stepped inside the large front room and was taken by the glamour of the place, the slave who had let him in announced his name to all.

"Mr. William Thomas," he said in a loud, clear voice.

Wil walked into the room where he was greeted by a number of people, some of whom he knew, others he did not. He was standing, talking to one of the men with whom he was acquainted. "Where is our host?" he asked.

The man nodded toward the other side of the room. "He's standing over there by the wall with that lovely young girl," he said. "She's his daughter."

Wil was taken by the beauty of the girl, even more than by the appearance of the father. He was suddenly overcome by a desire to meet the young lady. "Excuse me," he said, and he headed across the room. When he had reached his destination, he stopped and made a short bow. "Mr. Love?" he said. "I'm William Thomas."

"Mr. Thomas," said Love. "I'm delighted that you could make it. May I present my daughter, Sarah Jane? Sarah, this is Mr. Thomas."

"It's a great pleasure, Miss Love," said Wil.

"I'm pleased to meet you, sir," Sarah said.

Wil was pleased that Sarah was just about his height. Some of his previous loves had been taller than he was. When the musicians began to play, Wil asked Sarah if she would like to dance, and they danced several numbers together. All in all, Wil had a delightful evening. His head was swimming as he rode his horse back home. "Has my heart loved ere this?" he said out loud to the wind.

When he got home to Stekoih, he took off his hat and coat, lit the lamp, and sat down to read his Bible. Why he went to the Bible, he did not know, but he did find himself going to the Song of Solomon and reading the raciest passages.

He had a Bible in his cell, and he went to it. He took it with him back to his chair and opened it up to the Song of Solomon. He read aloud the following:

"As the lily among thorns, so is my love among the daughters." And then the female response. "As the apple tree among the trees of the wood, so is my beloved among the sons. I sat down under his shadow with great delight, and his fruit was sweet to my taste."

He put the book on the table and leaned back to relish the words and the delights that the words brought back to his mind. Soon he dropped off to sleep. When he awoke, his mind was someplace else entirely. He thought of the day that he received word of the battle at Baptist Gap.

An Indiana regiment of Union soldiers had been passing through the mountains of Union-friendly eastern Tennessee when they spotted Confederates down below. They quickly took up positions behind trees. Looking down on the trail where a Confederate lieutenant led his troops through the place known as Baptist Gap, they thought they had laid a perfect ambush. One Yankee soldier took careful aim at a Confederate rider who was wearing a turban on his head. He fired, and the rebel fell. "Attack," shouted Lieutenant Terrell. Then, led by Lieutenant Astoogatogeh, all of the Rebels dismounted and began charging up the mountainside, splitting the air with frightening yells. A Yankee rifle ball found Astoogatogeh's chest and he fell dead. The Cherokees were furious, for the lieutenant was well liked. He was a grandson of the great Junaluska. The Rebel yell was replaced by Cherokee war whoops, and the Union soldiers were suddenly terrified. They had expected the Rebels to dismount and hunt for cover, not to charge.

The Rebels ran straight up the steep mountainside into the ranks of the Yankees. If their weapons had already been fired, they used them as clubs, or they used knives or hatchets. Many of the Union soldiers ran through the trees for their lives. The Rebels, when they had killed an enemy, bent over the body and deftly removed the scalp.

As Wil recalled those events, events he had not witnessed but which had been reported to him, he did so with a mixture of delight and shame. He was delighted that his Cherokees had done such a fine job at the battle, but he was ashamed that they had reverted to their savage ways of scalping the dead. When Wil had the opportunity to address his Cherokee troops after that, he had delivered a lecture to them on the matter of scalping.

"It's a savage practice," he told them, "and I have been telling the state government and the white people, your neighbors, for years now that you have left behind your former savage ways. Now they will have this to reprimand us with. They will say that I have lied to them all this time. They will say that you all need to be shipped out of here and sent west with your brethren. I mean to make Christian soldiers of you, not savage soldiers. This business must not happen again."

Even as he delivered such an impassioned speech, he knew that what the Cherokees had done at Baptist Gap had struck terror into the hearts of their enemy. Any time a Union force met up with the Confederate Cherokees, they would remember what had happened that day. Thinking back on it now, he smiled. Now it suited him. He also remembered that in spite of his words, every time a Cherokee killed a Yankee in battle after that day, he stopped to take his scalp.

"Scare them to death," he shouted, sitting alone in his cell.

The door opened soon after that. George stuck his head in the room. "Mr. Thomas," he said, "is something wrong?"

"No," said Wil. "Nothing's wrong. I'm searching this cell for my knife. I know I have a knife in here, and when I find it, I'm going to use it to take your scalp from off your head. Ha! Here it is."

His hand was under the mattress on his bed. George's eyes opened wide; he backed up, slammed the door, and went running down the hallway screaming. Wil's hand came out from under the mattress—empty, of course. He sat down heavily in his chair and heaved a huge sigh. Why did he not have a knife? A Cherokee always had a knife. Where was his knife? Where was it?

In a few moments, a man in a black suit came into the room accompanied by George and two other white-suited men. George held back. The others stepped cautiously into the room.

"Mr. Thomas," said the black suit, "what is this we hear about a knife in your room?"

"A knife?" said Wil. "Why, I have no knife. They make me eat steak with a spoon. Have you ever tried to eat steak with a spoon? And by the way, who the hell are you anyway?"

"I'm the director of this institution. And you have threatened this man with a knife."

"Did he see a knife? George, did you see a knife?"

"No. I never saw it, but he yelled out that here it is, and that he was going to take my scalp. I know he lived with the Cherokees for years. I believed him."

"Mr. Thomas," said black suit, "why did you threaten George in that way?"

"Because he has been trying to poison me. That's why. I wouldn't kill him though. His scalp will satisfy me."

"That's nonsense, Mr. Thomas. No one is trying to poison you here."

"I believe that you are part of the conspiracy yourself. If I find my knife, I'll scalp you, too."

"Gentlemen," said black suit to the attendants, "search this room thoroughly. Make sure there is no knife or any other weapon in here."

The men began tearing apart Wil's room. They emptied every drawer. They tore the mattress from the bed. They threw all the clothes out of the closet. They even searched the clothes that Wil was wearing.

"Villains," said Wil. "Wretches. Would-be murderers. Yankee vermin."

"There is no weapon in this room, sir," George said to black suit.

"Very well," said black suit. "I want to hear no more such nonsense. And Mr. Thomas, I don't want to hear any more from you about scalping or about poison. Do you understand me?"

"I will be the pattern of all patience; I will say nothing."

The white suits began putting things back in their place, more or less. Things did not necessarily get replaced in the same drawers they were tossed out of, and the clothes in the closet were all rumpled. The mattress was back on the bed, but it was not straight, and the sheets were only tossed on top in a rumpled pile.

"Tell me something," said Wil.

"What?"

"How old am I?"

"I don't know," said black suit. "I'll have to check the files." Then he muttered as he walked through the door, "Yankees indeed."

Wil sat down when the men had left his room. He leaned back with a satisfied sigh. "His fruit was sweet to my taste," he said. He thought that he was at least seventy years old.

He remembered, though, his thirty-sixth birthday clearly. That was the day he had purchased the land where his mother lived on the Oconaluftee. That evening there had been a total eclipse of the moon. Some of the Indians had been a bit frightened by it, and it did seem eerie, Wil had to admit. At the time, he had remembered an old Cherokee story about a huge frog swallowing the moon. That, of course, explained its disappearance.

Wil recalled his thirty-sixth birthday as a good day. He had enjoyed seeing the eclipse of the moon and thinking about the moon being swallowed by a giant frog up in the sky; and it had, of course, been fortuitous that he had been able to secure the property for his home. He had wanted to move his mother from the Mount Prospect area for some time. Now he could do that.

Sitting in his cell, remembering these things, Wil thought that he should go back to Stekoih to visit his mother. He felt like it had been some time since he had done that. It was about time he went to see her again. And his Sarah, of course.

Sometimes the giant, malevolent frog came out in the daylight and was so bold as to swallow the sun. When that happened, the Cherokees were really frightened, because they depended so on the sun for warmth, to make their crops grow, and to give light during the daytime. They would run and get their rifles and fire them into the air. The women would get what steel pots and pans they had and bang on them, and everyone would scream and yell. All were trying to frighten the damned frog away to save the sun. Wil thought it was interesting that it always worked, for the frog would eventually regurgitate the sun, and the day would be bright again, and all would be well.

The poor moon had suffered a great deal throughout time. Wil recalled another old tale about the Moon and his sister the Sun. The Sun lived in the East. Her brother the Moon lived in the West. The young girl had a lover who came to visit her once a month when the Moon was in darkness, and he would always leave before daylight. They talked with one another, but because of the darkness, they could not see each other's faces. And he would not tell her his name. She wondered very much who he was.

One night when he came to see her, she slipped her hands into the ashes of the fireplace, and while they were making love, she rubbed his face with her hands. The next night when the Moon rose in the sky, she saw his face. It was covered with spots, and then she knew that it had been her brother who had been visiting her. The Moon was so embarrassed that his sister knew the truth, that ever since that event, he has kept as far away from her in the sky as he can.

Wil wondered if Mooney knew the Moon stories. Surely Swimmer had told them to him. He wondered when Mooney would come back to visit him again. He had liked Mooney, the fine young ethnologist. He wanted to see him again. Probably he would not. Probably one visit with the old mad man was enough for the dapper young gentleman from Washington. But did he know the Moon stories? Perhaps Wil should write him another letter.

He got out his paper and pen and carefully addressed a letter to Mr. James Mooney at the Bureau of American Ethnology in Washington, D.C., and he began to write.

My Dear Mr. Mooney,

I have been missing your good company. I enjoyed our last, our only, visit now ever since you left me here alone in my cell. No one comes to see me. My wife has not been here, nor have any of my children. Even my mother has not come to see me. I am very much alone in this cruel world.

I have a number of good things to tell you about the old time Cherokees, Mr. Mooney, and I have some questions to ask you. My keepers at this zoo have been trying to poison me for some time now, but I refuse to eat the food they bring me.

I want to know how old I am, but no one will tell me.

Please write to me soon and let me know when you will be coming round. I'm really craving some good company.

Your very humble servant,

Wil Usdi

Wil signed his name using the Cherokee syllabary. He reread the letter a few times, then folded it and placed it in a desk drawer. He would have to get George to post it for him. They did not allow him to perform any of these simple tasks for himself. They were afraid that he would run away. He might just do that, too. Run away to save himself.

CHAPTER SIX

Immortals

Wil had often heard it said by Cherokees that crazy persons were possessed by the devil. Cherokees, of course, had never believed in the devil until white missionaries had brought the belief to them. But then, Wil had been raised a Christian, and most of the Cherokees he knew were by this time all Christians, so perhaps the statement was not too wild. He sometimes felt like he was possessed by the devil. Who but the devil would confine him to this madhouse and make him live in a cell and be attended by a wretch like George?

He had never seen the devil nor heard him speak, but that was no proof. He could still be around. He could think of several people—all white—he had known over the years who might well have been the devil in disguise: those who had caused his three court-martials during the late war; some who had defrauded him in his stores; Abraham Lincoln, of course; and General Grant. All of them were devils.

But what if the old time Cherokees were right when they acknowledged no devil? What then? The other thing he had heard Cherokees say of crazy ones was that they were afflicted by the Nunnehi, the immortals or the People Who Live Anywhere. They lived in the high mountains of the old Cherokee country. In the bald mountains, the high peaks where no timber grows, they had a great many townhouses. They had one under the old

Nikwasi Mound in North Carolina, a place Wil had often seen in his life.

The Nunnehi were invisible unless they wanted to be seen, and when they did allow themselves to be seen, they looked just like other Indians. They loved to sing and dance. Often people wandering in the woods would hear singing and dancing, but when they moved toward the sounds, the sounds would move and be behind them. No one could ever find where the Nunnehi were. Once a Cherokee boy met a man in the forest, and the man took him home with him. A great many people were in the man's house, and they were all friendly with him. They kept the boy overnight, and the next day the man took him out to a road. "Follow this, and it will take you straight to your home," he said. As the boy walked down the road, he looked back over his shoulder and saw no house. He went on home and found the people there very happy and excited to see him. "We thought you were lost," said one. "Or drowned in the river," said another. Then the boy told them of his experience. "Oh," said an old one, "you were with the Nunnehi."

Once at Nottely Town there was a dance, and four beautiful women showed up. They danced for some time with the young men there, and then they left. Some of the young men wanted to know where the women had come from, so they followed them. They followed them to the river, and then they could see them no more. They had disappeared. "They were Nunnehi," one of the young men said.

He had heard the tale that old man Burnt Tobacco had been riding his horse, crossing the ridge from Nottely to Hemp Town, when he heard singing. It was strange, for there was no town nearby. He rode toward the sounds hoping to find who was singing. All of a sudden, the singing was coming from behind him. It scared him so badly that he flayed his horse and raced it all the way to Hemp Town.

A long time ago an invading force came into Cherokee country and laid to waste all of the lower settlements. They advanced into the mountains. The people of Nikwasi knew that the enemy were near. They put all of their women and children and old people into the townhouse for protection and readied themselves for a terrible battle. When they saw the enemy coming, they ran out to meet them, but soon they were being beaten back. Suddenly a stranger stood among them. He told the Nikwasi men to go on back, and he and his men would take care of the enemy. He looked like a Cherokee, so they thought that he had come from another Cherokee town to help them. They moved back out of the way, but as they neared their townhouse, they saw a great company of warriors come out of their mound as if through a door. One of the Nikwasi men said, "These are Nunnehi." As the battle raged on, the Nunnehi again became invisible. All the enemy could see were their war clubs in the air and their arrows flying at them. They fled in terror, but the Nunnehi pursued them to the Tuckasegee River. When there were only six of them left alive, they sat down and cried. The chief of the Nunnehis spared their lives, and told them to go home and tell their people what had happened to them there.

Sometimes the Nunnehi could be very helpful, but other times they could be most annoying, like when they felt mischievous. Like when they moved their dances around and frightened old Burnt Tobacco into nearly running his poor horse to death.

And Wil remembered clearly the time during the War Between the States, when some of his Cherokees who had been stationed at Franklin—the new town built where Nikwasi is located—had reported to him that a large force of Yankees was headed for them. All of a sudden, the town was guarded by hundreds of Confederate Cherokees, and the Yankees made a wide circle around it. The only place the soldiers could have come from was the Nikwasi Mound, just as the Nunnehi had done that time long ago, as told in the old tale. There was no attack. The Cherokees once again had been saved by the Nunnehi.

There was also the story of the old man who had been left nearly alone in his town because everyone else had gone to another town for a dance. He was outside chopping wood when a party of enemy Senecas came toward him. He threw his hatchet at them and ran toward his house for his gun, but before he could get there, a large body of strange warriors was already driving the enemy away. The old man went to thank them, but they disappeared. "Nunnehi," he said.

Wil wondered if the Nunnehi, who had helped him before, could be causing his madness now. Perhaps he had done something to offend them, something that he was unaware of. They might have taken his rifle or his saber. That would explain why he could not find them. Perhaps they were working to make him crazy.

But he felt like Cudjo should be able to help him. Where was Cudjo? He had not seen the faithful old man for some time now. He couldn't remember when he last saw Cudjo. Cudjo had been the slave of old Yonaguska for as long as Wil Usdi knew. When Yonaguska had died, he had left Cudjo to Wil. Cudjo was totally trustworthy. When Wil went on his long trips away from home, he left Cudjo to take care of his mother, to make sure she had all the firewood she needed and to help her with her chores around the house and anything else. Of course, he also told the men who ran the store for him to give her anything she needed or wanted, so Mother was well taken care of. But he did not know what he would have done all those years without old Cudjo. Why, Cudjo was so trustworthy that once Wil had sent him with $350 on a trip alone to pay off a creditor.

Of course, as time went by, he bought other slaves to help with the work around the stores and around the house. They were invaluable. Now and then, Wil also sold slaves, always for a profit; but he did not engage in much of that business. It was not a particularly worthy way for an honest businessman to make a living, trafficking in human beings. He had used four slaves in purchasing his land at Stekoih, the land where his mother now lived. He had paid for the property with the slaves and some money.

The slaves had been a good investment. They helped at the stores. They were especially helpful when wagonloads of goods that Wil had purchased in far-flung places such as Athens or Augusta, Georgia, or Charleston, South Carolina, arrived at the stores and needed to be unloaded. Thinking of Charleston reminded him of a particularly frightening event in his life.

He had been riding in an open railroad car to Charleston when the car suddenly derailed. The jolt was terrifying, and then the car had overturned. Wil and the other passengers in the car had been flung far and wide. Luckily, the train had been traveling slowly, so no one was killed or seriously injured; but flying through the air unexpectedly, and even more, the landing and tumbling on the hard ground had been a real trauma.

As soon as he had realized that he had no broken bones, he had stood up and dusted himself off. He had then gone to help others, especially the women. When he was assured that no one was hurt, he looked to the train. It had stopped not far ahead. Happily, the open car was not too heavy, and the passengers had helped the train crew to right the car and get it back onto the tracks. It had been an experience he would not forget.

He remembered that at the time he had longed for Cudjo and a few others of his slaves to be there to help. Where the hell was Cudjo? He would be able to tell Wil how old he was. He would also fetch him his pipe, some tobacco, and some means of lighting it. The criminals who ran this madhouse would not let him have such things. That was another reason he longed to stab them with a fork, but only if he could not find his knife or his sword, which those damned mischievous immortals had hidden from him.

If he could only see Cudjo, he knew that Cudjo would bring him a knife and a fork to eat with and his rifle or a pistol, a knife for stabbing, or his sword. Cudjo would break him out of this damnable place. He would have a saddled horse ready and waiting outside on which Wil could make good his escape. He longed for that time. It was even good to just think about it. And if the guards came after him, he would shoot them down like dogs. Cudjo would, of course, have also brought him his gun.

Why didn't Mother come to see him? He longed to see her. He had been good to her over the long years, and she knew it. She should come to see him. And his wife and his other women? They should all come around. His children, too. He did miss them all. Perhaps it was because he had been gone from home so much, traveling on business for the Cherokees or for his store. And the war. That had kept him away for a long time. All that business had kept him away from home for long periods of time. There was that one time he had spent three years in Washington City, three long years.

And what had it been for? He tried to recall, but it was muddled in his brain. It had something to do with the Removal

Treaty, he thought. Yes. The treaty was in need of being ratified, and the Congress was dragging its feet. Wil wanted the treaty to be ratified, for he saw it as a means of getting some money for the Luftee Indians. Yonaguska had signed a contract with Wil saying that if Wil got money for the Indians, then Wil would get a percentage of that money for himself. While he was there in Washington, Wil had met Major Ridge, the leader of the Treaty Party, and they had become friends.

But Ridge was a fierce opponent of Principal Chief John Ross, who was doing all he could to keep the treaty from being ratified. Ross had been telling all the Cherokees that they could stay on their lands. Wil thought that the Cherokees would be moved no matter what, but if they moved under the terms of the treaty, they would receive money for their land. The Luftee Indians were Cherokees also, so they would deserve a share of that money. He meant to have it for them.

He further wanted the money paid to him as agent of the Luftee Indians. Wil would get their money, and he would then go back to North Carolina and buy land for them. He would hold that land in his name, and they would live on it and have full use of it. He had much work to do. He also had to assure that the Luftee Indians would have their rights respected by the federal government and be allowed to remain in North Carolina as citizens of the state and of the United States.

Further, he had to get Ridge to promise that the Luftee Indians would not be deprived of their rights under the treaty by the Cherokee Nation. He was successful on the two major points. Ridge agreed and the government agreed that the Luftee Indians would not be removed. He did not, however, collect all of the money that he felt was due his clients. That would take longer. It would take more work. And there would be those who would attack Wil, accusing him of using the Indians' money to his own benefit. After all, the land he purchased for them as the years went on was all recorded in his name.

Wil also bought land for himself with his own money, and he claimed that some of the land he purchased for the Indians had also been paid for with his own money. How was anyone to tell what land he had gotten for the Indians and what for himself? It was a vicious trap he had gotten himself into, but there was no other way to acquire land for the Indians.

"I am a man more sinned against than sinning."

Recalling those days, Wil felt a deep-seated resentment arise from inside him toward those whites who promulgated that law. They thought that Indians were less than human beings, and Wil felt sure that, if anything, Indians were more human than were the whites. He felt as sure of that as of anything else he had left in his withering brain.

CHAPTER SEVEN

The Storm

George knocked at the door and stepped into the room with food on a tray. "Supper, Mr. Thomas," he said.

"I'll go to supper i' th' morning," said Wil.

"Well," said George, "I'll just leave this here for you." He put the tray down on the table and left the room. Wil turned his head to look across the room at the tray of poisoned food that waited there for him. He turned his head back to look out the window again. It was raining again, just a slight, drizzling rain. There was a sudden, loud clap of thunder that caused Wil to jump. He stood up with an effort, for his legs were hurting him, and hurried over to the window to look out. The rain began to come down harder and faster. Soon it was pounding. There was more lightning and thunder.

"Blow, winds, and crack your cheeks," Wil yelled out the window.

> Rage, blow,
> You cataracts and hurricanoes, spout
> Till you have drench'd our steeples, drown'd the cocks,
> You sulph'rous and thought-executing fires,
> Vaunt-couriers of oak-cleaving thunderbolts,
> Singe my white head! And thou, all-shaking thunder,
> Strike flat the thick rotundity o' th' world,
> Crack nature's moulds, all germens spill at once,
> That makes ingrateful man!

The door opened again, and George stuck his head in. "Mr. Thomas?"

"Away! Away!" shouted Wil, and George disappeared and slammed the door shut. Another loud clap of thunder sounded, much closer than the first. Wil thought that it was damn near on top of the building.

"Rumble thy bellyful!" he roared. "Spit, fire! spout, rain!"

> here I stand, your slave,
> A poor, infirm, weak, and despis'd old man.
> . . .
> So old and white as this. O! O! 't is foul!

All of a sudden, he was calm again. He stared out at the pounding rain for a moment or two. Then he turned to walk back into the room. He was moving toward his chair when his legs almost gave out underneath him. He cried out and grabbed for the table, just saving himself from a tumble. He carefully made his way back to his chair and sat down heavily in it. He leaned back and breathed several deep breaths.

"The body's delicate," he said. "The tempest in my mind"

> Doth from my senses take all feeling else
> Save what beats there.
> . . .
> O, that way madness lies; let me shun that;
> No more of that.

The lightning flashed outside the window, lighting up the black sky in flashes, and when it did, the dark cell was also lighted. Then came another roaring blast of thunder that actually shook the building. Wil Usdi dove to the floor and covered his head with his hands.

"God damn those Yankee cannons," he cried out.

He had been transposed to the field of battle in front of his legion. Cannonballs and rifle shells were exploding all around him. He reached for a nearby chair and grabbed it to help hoist himself up onto his feet. His legs were hurting and his ears were roaring. Suddenly, he began rushing around the room, flinging things this way and that, searching madly for his weapons. Where were they? His sword? His rifle? His pistols? Where the hell had they got to?

He awoke in a cold sweat. He remembered the thunderstorm, and he remembered being frightened. But why had he been frightened? He had never been frightened of thunder, especially since old Yonaguska had told him that Thunder was the friend of the Cherokees.

He had been fighting the war again. He remembered that. He thought about all the time he and his legion had spent in the vicinity of Knoxville, there in the eastern part of Tennessee, a strange place, especially during the war. Tennessee was a Southern state and had gone for the Confederacy, but the eastern part of the state did not agree. The people there were mostly northern sympathizers. It had been an uncomfortable place for a Confederate legion to be stationed.

Union forces burned five bridges, and the rebellious east Tennesseans grew bold. Colonel Thomas recalled the night that ten pro-Union men approached the bridge at Strawberry Plains, the bridge that he and his legion had been charged to guard. One of the pro-Union men struck a match to better see, but no sooner had he done so than a shot rang out, and he fell wounded. Keelan, the Confederate guard who had fired the shot, sprang on the wounded saboteur, but the man's partner jumped on Keelan and slashed him with his knife. Keelan continued to fight, though, even when two more Union men came to join in the fray. He fought them off with his pistol butt and a knife. Someone fired a shot, and Keelan was hit in the arm. Keelan fought with such fury that the four Unionists at last ran away. Colonel Thomas was very proud of that man Keelan. He had single-handedly saved the bridge.

He then thought about the time the Unionist home guard at Sevierville had jailed a few of his Indians. When he was given the news, he had become furious and had taken two hundred of his men to Sevierville and surprised the guard at the jail. The guard threw down his weapons immediately and raised his hands high in the air. Then Wil Usdi directed several of his biggest Indians to break down the jail door. They bashed into it with their shoulders and kicked it with their feet. At long last, they broke the door open and rescued their comrades. They then surprised other home guards, capturing about sixty of them. Taking their prisoners and their prisoners' weapons and ammunition with them, the Cherokees returned to their camp successful and triumphant. Wil Usdi puffed up recalling that event.

The next morning in their camp near Gatlinburg, the Cherokees had been preparing their breakfast when they were surprised by a sudden attack. They quickly formed skirmish lines and fired several volleys at the Yankees, holding them back for maybe an hour. At last they were forced to retreat. The Cherokees ran up the mountainside, scattering in the thick woods. The Yankees were soon frustrated because they were unable to keep up with the Cherokees in that dense terrain. They gave up the chase and went back down to the camp where they devoured the corn cakes the Cherokees had been preparing for their breakfast.

In western North Carolina, as in east Tennessee, there were large numbers of Union sympathizers. There were also deserters from both armies. Often these deserters came together and formed outlaw gangs, posing as Union home guards. They were mostly known as bushwhackers. Captain Goldman Bryson led one group of maybe 150 men. They sacked Murphy, and they were busy recruiting for the Union. General Vaughan was ordered to track down and destroy Bryson's raiders. Vaughan and his troops caught up with the raiders, killed two, and captured seventeen. The rest, including Bryson, escaped.

Colonel Thomas sent Lieutenant Taylor and one Cherokee company to aid Vaughan, but the company arrived after Bryson's escape. Taylor and the Cherokees tracked Bryson and one other man to the area near Bryson's own home. Taylor fired a shot at Bryson, who was on foot. He staggered but continued running. Other Cherokees fired, and Bryson was hit several times before he fell. Some of the Cherokees stripped the body and put on his bloody clothes.

Wil Usdi liked recalling incidents from the war when his Cherokees were successful in defeating the Yankees. He tried not to think of other, less successful moments from that bloody conflict.

A few moments later George brought Wil his meal; Wil thanked him, and he took the meal and began to eat. George was astonished, but he said nothing. The old man, he thought, may be somewhat improved.

"This is good," Wil said. "Very good. Thank you, George."

"You're welcome, Mr. Thomas," said George.

The doctor came in to see Wil later that same day. "How are you feeling today, Mr. Thomas?" he asked.

"I feel well," said Wil. "Quite well indeed. Won't you sit down, Doctor?"

"Thank you," said the doctor, and he took a seat.

"I understand that you ate your food today. That's good news."

"Yes. I was hungry. I don't know what's been the matter with me lately. I think perhaps I've been a little bit crazy. Do you think that's it?"

The doctor chuckled. "Perhaps," he said. "I should say, rather, somewhat disturbed."

"That's a kindlier way to put it, I suppose," said Wil.

They continued making small talk for a few more minutes before the doctor excused himself and left the room. "I'll come back to see you tomorrow or the next day," he said as he left.

Wil mused about the meeting for a few minutes. He thought the doctor was a nice man. In fact, he told himself, they're all nice here. They treat me rather well, even when I'm into one of those mad spells I get. But I'm all right now. I'm perfectly all right. If I went crazy for a time, I've gotten over it now. I'll eat all the meals they bring me—with my spoon. I'll not complain about anything. I'll not shout and act crazy. I'll just be a perfectly normal human being. I'm all right.

Two days later the doctor said that he had recovered and could go back home. He was seventy years old.

CHAPTER EIGHT

Back Home

For a time Wil was perfectly happy back home at Stekoih in the bosom of his family. Sarah was as lovely as ever in his eyes. Young William Holland Thomas, Jr., was fast becoming a man. Wil was proud of the boy. His daughter, Sallie Love, was growing into a beautiful young woman girl. William Hyde was there also, an offspring of Wil's clandestine affair with Catharine years earlier. Angelina, the daughter of Kanaka, was in the fold as well. Sarah was wonderful to allow Wil to care for his illegitimate children in that way. Cudjo was still hanging around, still faithful to Wil and the memory of Yonaguska.

The children hung around him, calling him Pa, and making a fuss over him in such a way as to cause him to feel very important indeed. Perhaps he was in their eyes. After all, he was their father, and he had been a most important man in his lifetime: almost an Indian chief, a state senator, and a Confederate colonel. Sometimes they asked him to tell tales of his days of fame.

But, he thought, that was all in his past. He was now an almost-forgotten old man. Who remembered his days of glory, his fiery speeches, his military charges, his challenges to the federal government on behalf of his Cherokee clients? Who recalled that it was he, and he alone, who had acquired the land for the Eastern Cherokees to live on? Who was responsible for their very existence in the state of North Carolina? Who but his children and his beloved wife, his Sarah?

His mother was still around, too, nearly one hundred years old. She was getting feeble now and did not seem well. It saddened Wil to see her thus, but he knew that the time had come. She had lived a long and useful life, and he wanted only to see her well taken care of, to see her relax and enjoy what was left of her life. He knew she was responsible for his life in more ways than one. Not only had she given him life in the first place, she had also educated him and secured for him his first position. He owed her all, and he told her so as often as he got the chance. He loved her so much.

Now and then he allowed his mind to wander back to his early years at the cabin on Raccoon Creek, near Mount Prospect. Well, they were calling it Waynesville now. He would recall in detail the pleasant times he'd had there with his mother. He would remember how lovely and how young she had been, and then he would curse the ravages of time, thinking about the contrast between the young mother he recalled and the mother he was seeing before him now.

After such thoughts, he would jerk his mind back to the present, for he believed that the wandering mind assuredly led to madness. He did not want to think about the past. It was difficult, though, not to think about it. There was so much to think about, and so much of it included pleasant memories. But no. Think on the present, or even on the future. He would look at his children and think how proud of them he was, and he would wonder about their futures. What would become of them? Had he left them anything to build on?

He would then become ashamed. He knew that his finances were a mess. He knew that his debtors were after him from all sides. He realized that he was secured from their pressures by his madness. He was well aware that people were after his landholdings to pay for his debts, including some of the land-holdings that he had purchased for the Cherokees with the Cherokees' own money. He tried to get involved in some of those squabbles, but it was difficult for him to sort out the dealings in his mind. He hoped that the Cherokees at least would find a competent lawyer to help them hang onto their lands.

One evening he was sitting in a comfortable chair in the parlor, looking at the piano he had purchased some years earlier for his Sarah. She played beautifully, and she had longed for a piano. He had gotten one for her, and he loved to hear her play on it. It was late, though, and Wil was sleepy. So was everyone else, and they all got ready for bed. Wil felt sorry for himself as he lay in bed beside his lovely wife that night. He longed to disrobe her and make mad, passionate love to her, but he knew that he was unable to do so. The longing was so great that Wil could not sleep. What a terrible thing it is, he thought, to be too old to do something, but not too old to long for it. He had no idea how long he lay awake, but at last he did fall asleep.

When he woke up in the morning, it was late. Everyone else was already up, dressed, and finished with their breakfast. As soon as Wil got up, Sarah poured him a cup of coffee. "I'll have your breakfast in just a minute, Wil," she said. "There's no rush, my sweet," he said. "I just slept too late is all."

"Well, you must have needed the sleep, dear. I'll get your breakfast now."

As he ate the meal of fried eggs and good, sugar-cured ham that Sarah had prepared for him, he thought about the meals they fed him at the madhouse. Why couldn't they cook like this? Why did their eggs and ham and steak and bread and potatoes all taste the same? "Sarah, my love," he said, "you are the most wonderful cook in the entire South."

She cleared away his dishes as he finished with them, and he watched her with a smile on his face. At last he stood up from the table to go into the parlor, and as he did, he moaned out loud. "What is it, Wil?" said Sarah.

"It's just my legs," he said. "They're hurting again."

"Bad?"

"Something awful."

Moving from one chair to another, he made his way into the other room and to the comfortable chair he wanted to sit in. Sarah followed him, a look of concern on her face. Wil dropped into the chair. He looked over at the piano. "Sarah," he said, "will you play something for me? I love to hear you play, and it's been so long. Play for me."

"Not now, Wil," she said. "I burned my hand cooking breakfast this morning, and it hurts too bad. Maybe later."

Wil sprang up too quickly it seemed for a man whose legs were paining him. "I said play," he commanded.

She looked at him with fear and worry.

"I can't. Not now."

Over in the corner of the room, some tools were propped against the wall beside the door. One of them was a small hatchet. Wil rushed over to it and grabbed it. Then he hurried to Sarah's side, and he raised the hatchet above her head. "I said play," he growled. "Play for me, if you know what's good for you."

Just at that moment, Will Jr. came into the room. He stopped with a terrified look on his face, and then he ran over to his father and grabbed the wrist of the hand that held the hatchet high. "Pa," he cried out. "What's wrong with you? Stop it. Let me have that hatchet. Let go of it."

From the other room, Angelina heard the ruckus and came rushing into the room to see what was happening. When she saw her half-brother struggling with her father over the hatchet held above Sarah's head, she jerked open the front door and screamed out, "William! William, come quick! We need you!" William Hyde was in the house in a few seconds. He took in the situation in a moment and hurried to help Will Jr. Soon the hatchet was wrenched from Wil's hand and tossed to the floor, and Wil was restrained, one son holding each arm.

"Pa, what's wrong with you?" said William Hyde. "Are you crazy?" Wil turned his head sharply and looked into Hyde's eyes, his own eyes seeming to blaze with what did indeed look like insanity.

They sent Angelina for a length of rope, and then they bound Wil's hands behind his back. They were afraid to leave him loose. He sat sulking in his chair with his hands tied that way, while his son Will Jr., went out for the sheriff. It was a while before they got back to the house. "How much will you charge me?" Will Jr., was saying.

"Thirty-three dollars ought to do it," the sheriff said.

Will Jr., dug in his pockets and came up with two twenty-dollar bills, which he handed to the sheriff. The sheriff looked at them and tucked them into a shirt pocket. "I'll have to get you your change later," he said.

"That's all right."

The sheriff had driven a buggy to the house at Stekoih, and he and the two sons hustled Wil out to the buggy and loaded him into it. "Don't hurt him, Sheriff," Sarah said.

"Don't worry, Miz Thomas," said the sheriff.

Sarah stepped up close to Wil and put a hand on his arm. She stared into his face. "I'm sorry, Wil," she said. "I hoped you'd be able to stay home with us this time—at last."

"Good bye," said Wil.

CHAPTER NINE

Chief, Senator, Colonel

They put Wil back into his same old room—the cell, he called it. In a very peculiar way, he was glad to be back. He almost hated himself when he realized that strange fact. But the cell was comfortable. It was familiar to him. He knew where everything was. He knew when his meals would be brought to him. He knew what they would taste like. They would all taste the same, no matter what they were called. His clothes had been brought back along with him, including his old Confederate uniform—but not his weapons. His notebooks and pencils had been brought along as well. The long drive in the wagon with the sheriff had calmed him down, and he no longer felt crazy.

He knew though that he was mad, mad as a hatter, but he was having a lucid period now. He wondered how long it might last. He hoped it would stay with him. Even though he was comfortable in these surroundings, he would have liked to be with his wife and his mother. He loved them both very much, but they said he had threatened Sarah with a hatchet. He hated that. It was hard to believe, but William and Will Jr. both said it was true. They said they'd had to restrain him and take the hatchet away from him and go for the sheriff.

The last thing that Wil would ever want to do was to harm Sarah or even to frighten her. It was awful to think of Sarah being frightened of him. Sarah, the love of his life. He had told her that he lived for her love, and that was all. He lived for her love. How could he frighten her like that? To wave a hatchet over her head. God, he was so glad that his sons had been there to stop him. Would he, he wondered, have actually struck her with the weapon? Had his sons saved her life? Saved Sarah from Wil?

He belonged in this place, he told himself. There was no doubt about it. This was where he must stay. What if he managed to convince the doctors once again that he was sane? What if they sent him home again? What if, once he got back home, he slipped back into his madness? And what if the next time the boys weren't around when they were needed? What if he should kill someone? It was too horrible to think about. He did not want to go home again.

The chief! The senator! The Confederate colonel! To end his life in a state madhouse! It was the supreme irony of his life. He thought about writing the story of his life. That would be a way to pass the time. Instead, George came in with his meal. Which meal was it? He did not know. He had no idea what time of day it was, and as far as the meal was concerned it did not matter, for they all tasted the same.

"Hello, George," he said. "Is it noon already? Is this my breakfast you've brought me?"

"No, sir. It's evening. It's suppertime."

"Oh, then you've brought my lunch. Thank you."

George put the meal down on the table.

"Is my spoon there?"

"Yes."

"And my coffee?"

"Yes."

"Then everything is as it should be." He picked up the spoon and dug a bite out of something. He didn't know what it was. He ate it. "Oh, yes, it's the same taste I remember. Everything is as it should be. Thank you, George."

George left the room, and Wil ate everything on the plate. Then he drank the coffee down. The coffee is good, he thought. That's the one thing they know how to do in the kitchen in this place. They make good coffee. He finished the coffee, and he wanted another cup. He was about to get up and go to the door to call out for George to fetch him some more when he saw the carafe. He picked it up and tipped it into his coffee cup. Something came running out that looked like coffee. He picked up the cup and tasted the stuff. It was coffee. This was a new touch, this carafe with extra coffee. He managed to have two more cups of coffee before it was all gone.

In a few moments George returned to take the tray and dishes away. "George," said Wil, "the extra coffee was an excellent touch."

"Oh? I'm glad that you liked it."

"I liked it very much."

"Would you like for me to bring you some more?"

"No, thank you, George. It was just the right amount. Will you bring it like that at all meals now?"

"I'll be certain to, sir," George said.

As George left the room, Wil said to himself, it's small things like that that make all the difference in a man's life. I think I'll be happy here.

He went to sleep thinking about Sarah, and crying.

While he slept, he dreamed. He found himself back on Raccoon Creek fishing with his mother; she was sitting on the bank reading a book. He was having a wonderful day, and he was catching fish, too. He had a mess of perch. They were tasty little devils, but they were chock-full of tiny bones. You had to be really careful eating them or you might swallow a tiny, sharp bone. After a little while, he was eating them. The smell and the taste were both delicious.

The next thing he knew, he was playing stickball with Cherokees, and he caught a high-flying ball that came plummeting down toward his head. He reached up with both his sticks and snatched it right out of the air. There were three or four players from the opposing team running right at him. He took a few quick steps to dodge them, and then he spotted one of his own men down near the goal line. He made a mighty toss with his sticks and released the ball. It flew high above everyone's head and arced right down to his target. The man caught the ball and ran it between the goal sticks. A score!

He found himself next in Washington, where he was arguing with some politicians about the money due to the Eastern Cherokees from their share of the payment for all the Eastern Cherokee land. They were resisting his arguments, but he was firm. He was arguing like an old-fashioned Greek orator, or better yet, he was talking like a great Cherokee speaker, but the dream ended before the argument was resolved, and he was in a uniform leading a charge against a huge, well-mounted, well-armed contingent of Yankee soldiers. Bullets whizzed by his head and tore at his clothes. Shells exploded all around.

He rode into the midst of the enemy, swinging his sword left and right, slicing his enemies all around. Blood was flying through the air and splattering even unwounded men, so that everyone he could see was bloody, either with their own blood or someone else's. Then he was alone on the bloody, fiery field. He was surrounded by Yankees, some aiming revolvers at him, some aiming rifles, and some pointing bayonets. They all started moving in toward him. They came closer and closer, and then he woke up. He sat up in a cold sweat. His dreams had all been based on real events in his life, but some of them were fed as well by his wild imagination.

He stood up and found both his legs hurting. He had a roaring in his ears. He staggered toward his water bowl. It was empty. He picked up the water pitcher and poured some water into the bowl. Then he dipped a rag in the water and used it to wash his face. It was still dark outside, but he wanted to be up. He was not sleepy any longer, and he certainly did not want to dream again. The Yankees might just finish him off if he did.

> To die, to sleep;
> To sleep: perchance to dream: ay, there's the rub;
> For in that sleep of death what dreams may come
> When we have shuffled off this mortal coil,
> Must give us pause:

He could always find comfort in the words of the Bard, more even than in the words of the Bible. He felt guilty at that thought, when he said those words, but the Bard's words were true, as true as they could be. "Truer words were never spoken," he said out loud. "Never!"

Then he felt like he should read the Bible. He rummaged around his room until he found it. He sat down and thumbed through, looking for—what? He wasn't at all sure what he was looking for. Just something to make him feel safer after what he had said? There is supposed to be comfort in the Good Book, he thought. But his mind would not focus on the Good Book, and that angered him. He slapped the book shut and flung it across the room.

Why did I do that? He thought. Surely I will be consigned to the fires of hell for that horrid act. Why do I not have any visitors? What is wrong with me? What have I done to deserve this punishment?

He recalled the Battle of Piedmont in Virginia during the war. He remembered that he had lost the command of his legion and was in a dreadful, despondent state. A large federal force was expected to move into Virginia to attempt to take over the Shenandoah Valley. The Thomas Legion and other Confederate troops were ordered into the valley, and, interestingly enough, Colonel Thomas, who was in western North Carolina, was restored to his command. He wished that he were with his legion in Virginia now.

When the Yankees moved into the valley, the Confederates were in a poor place to receive them. They fought valiantly, but they were whipped. They scattered into the woods with Yankees in pursuit. The Thomas Legion, chased into the wooded mountains, unexpectedly decided to turn and fight. They did so, and they fought valiantly, this time whipping the Union troops. Then, having taken their revenge, they finished their retreat. This time, though, they had some prisoners. The big Battle of Piedmont was a defeat, but the Thomas Legion had won itself a small victory.

Wil Usdi was proud of his legion. Up until that time, they had been made sport of. It had been said of them that they never fought in major battles. They stood guard over bridges. They ran around in the mountains of North Carolina. But now they had whipped some Yankees and captured a few prisoners. They had proved themselves to be brave fighting men. And he was proud. He only wished that he had been there with them to share in that victory.

He had not been with them, of course. He had only heard the details of the battle from others who had been there, and he had read reports of it in the newspapers. He had been robbed of the privilege of being there by political shenanigans, and he had some growing hatreds for a few self-aggrandizing, swollen-headed politicians who were posing as military men. Damn their souls.

Furious all of a sudden, Wil rushed about the room searching for his sword. He knocked over tables and chairs. He rummaged through his closet, tossing everything in there out onto the floor. At last, his legs causing him tremendous pain, he threw himself onto the bed. He covered his ears with his hands in a vain attempt to stop the horrible roaring in them.

"I am not mad," he said out loud. "Not mad. I cannot be mad. No. I am but mad north-north-west. When the wind is southerly, I know a hawk from a handsaw."

Then he began to weep. "I want to see my Sarah," he said. "I need her. I love her more than my life. She is my life. She is all. Without her I am nothing. Without her—perhaps I am mad."

He tried to recall the many times he had been to the halls of Congress on behalf of the Cherokees, and how many times he had won his point and succeeded in getting their money for them or permission for them to remain on their lands—his land—in North Carolina. The details escaped him. He reached back for some bits of his successful campaigning for the North Carolina Senate and for the things he had won for western North Carolina while he was a senator. The only thing he could recall was voting to establish the madhouse. He laughed out loud. What irony was in that? "God damn me," he shouted.

The war was the next thing. He remembered resigning from the Senate in order to raise his legion, but again, he could not recall any details. He knew he had done it, but how? How had he accomplished that and the many other great things he had done in his life? He had a vague feeling that he was a great man, but he couldn't be certain of that, for he could not recollect how anything had been accomplished. Perhaps those things had just fallen into his lap. Perhaps he had just been lucky.

Then an old stickball game came into his head, and he recalled it in great detail. He had stripped to nothing but a pair of shorts. The players had already been taken to the water and been scratched. The scratch marks down Wil Usdi's back and along the backs of his legs were still dripping fresh drops of blood. He was anxious for the action to begin. The team was lined up facing their opponents, a team of Creeks with whom they had been arguing over a piece of land. The outcome of the game would determine ownership of the land in question. Both teams whooped loudly, trying to intimidate the others. The driver took up the ball and held it high over his head. Both teams were ready.

Then the driver dropped his hand and flung the ball high in the air. All players crowded around him and reached high with their ballsticks, watching the ball as it arced high and then began to descend. One Cherokee player had worked himself around behind the crowd toward the end of the field where the Cherokees' goal waited. Another Cherokee player in the crowd reached up with his stick and swatted the ball as it came down. He drove it right at the lone Cherokee behind the crowd, who was waiting for it. That player reached with both his sticks, caught the ball between the webbed ends of the sticks, and turned and ran with all his might toward the Cherokee goal.

But the Creeks had a fast runner on their team, and he caught up with the Cherokee and tackled him to the ground. As the Cherokee fell, he looked to his right to see one of his teammates running there. He flipped the ball toward that player, who caught it and continued running. The Creeks all ran after him, but he outran them and made it between the goal sticks for a score. The Cherokees all jumped and whooped in joy.

The driver again got the ball and tossed it high. This time there was a scramble for the ball, and a Creek player came out of the crowd clutching it in his fist. He ran hard for his goal, and he was running directly toward Wil Usdi. Wil bent his knees and braced himself. The Creek runner did not even try to dodge Wil. Probably because Wil was so small, the man figured he could run right over him. Their bodies collided with a loud smash, and Wil straightened up with the Creek runner draped over his shoulder. He put his hands on the man's thighs and shoved hard, straightening his legs at the same time, and he flung the man high over his head. The Creek landed hard, flat on his back. The air was all knocked out of his lungs, so he lay there helpless. He could not move as he sucked hard for air.

Three Cherokees immediately pounced on him, grappling for the ball. One of the Cherokees ripped the ball from the Creek's hand just as seven more Creeks came on the scene. As the Cherokee turned to run, a Creek hit him hard over the head with a ballstick. The Cherokee fell, dropping the ball. Another Creek grabbed up the ball and ran it across the Creek goal for a score. The Creeks whooped and hollered. One Creek turned his back to the Cherokees and lifted his loincloth, exposing his bare buttocks to them. In return, the Cherokees all imitated the loud gobbling of turkeys. The man who had been hit on the head staggered toward the sidelines, carrying both ballsticks in one hand. Blood was running down the side of his head.

Wil then focused on the man who had hurt that player. His thoughts were no longer on the ball. He wanted to get revenge for the injury. He tried to keep himself somewhere near that

Creek player. At last Wil was knocked down, and instead of getting quickly back up to his feet, he lay there as if he had been stunned. The crowd was rushing past, chasing the ball, and the object of Wil's vengeance came running very closely past him. Wil waited for just the right minute and smacked the man across the shins with all his might, making him scream in pain and fall over on his face. He rolled around crying out and rubbing his shins with both hands. Wil got to his feet and ran after the crowd. He was feeling quite smug, until a big Creek reached out a long arm and wrapped it around him, pulling him close into his own body and holding him there.

Wil struggled, trying to break loose from the man's hold, but it was no use. He could not do it. He jabbed the man in his ribs with his elbows, but when he did, the man conked him on the head with his ballstick. At last, helpless, Wil stood still, and the man still held on to him tightly. Wil realized that he was out of the game for good. The man's whole and entire motive seemed to be to hold Wil out of the game. Now all he could do was watch as the game rushed back and forth in front of his eyes, as the Cherokees and then the Creeks scored points.

It was a high-scoring game. For a time the Cherokees would be ahead, and then the Creeks would catch up and leap ahead. Finally, the Cherokees won the game. The screaming knew no bounds. Wil twisted his head in an attempt to look in the face of his large captor. "The game is over now," he said. "Let me go." The big Creek lifted Wil up in his arms like a baby, looked down at him, and then tossed him aside like a sack of garbage. Wil landed hard on the ground but stood up quickly, and then whooped and hollered as he ran to join his triumphant teammates in their celebration.

CHAPTER TEN

Big Breakout Attempt

Wil was exhausted after the big stickball game. He sat down on the edge of his bed and rubbed his thighs, but in a moment he realized there was something wrong. Where had this bed come from? And he did not remember changing into these clothes. He could not recall anyone having kidnapped him following the game, but something like that must have happened. "God damn them," he said out loud. He started to shout it out, but he checked himself. That was not a good idea. He must keep quiet. He went to his closet where he found a long, black coat. He put that on.

He walked quietly over to the door and opened it slowly. Then he edged into the opening and looked out carefully into the long hallway. He looked both directions and saw no one. Good. He stepped out into the hall and walked quickly, but quietly, down to the end. There was a door that led outside, and, to his right, another door that led into the dining hall and lounge area. He was not hungry, and he did not want to go in there. The lounge was usually full of a bunch of old nuts anyhow. He opened the door to the outside and stepped out, leaning against the brick wall just beside the door.

He could feel the cold bricks even through the big coat. They felt good to him. He felt he could stay there for a long time, but then, if he did that, they might locate him. Goddamn Yankees, he thought. He looked around. There was a big yard and, around it, a tall fence. He knew there was a gate in the fence directly in line with the main front door of the building, which was around the corner from where he leaned against the wall. He made his way slowly and carefully down to the corner of the building and peeked around. He saw no one. It was late at night. Wil wasn't sure of the time. He had no watch, and he did not give a damn about the time of day anyhow. It was a dark night; that was all he needed to know.

He wanted to go home and sleep in his own bed. He wanted to see his lovely Sarah. He missed her so, and he loved her so much. He could not remember when the last time was he had seen her. He remembered, though, that she had said she wished he could stay home with her. He wished the same thing, more than he could say. If he went home to see her, he would see his children as well, and that, too, would be nice. He would like to see his children. And his faithful slave Cudjo. It would be good to see ole Cudjo. Cudjo would do anything for Wil. Wil figured that he could tell Cudjo to kill that damned doctor who kept saying that he was crazy, and Cudjo would do it.

How would he do it? Would he just pick the doctor up and break his back? Would he come up behind him and snap his neck? He might slip a knife in slowly between his ribs. Or Wil could let him use one of his pistols, and Cudjo might just fire a round into the man's stupid head. The doctor was so stupid; it would be no loss to the world. He was wasting time, though. He began edging his way toward the main entrance to the building. "But why am I doing this?" he asked himself.

It's much farther if I go to the door. I can just make a bee-line for the gate from here. It's closer that way. And so he leaned out from the wall, took several deep breaths and ran as hard as he could run. About halfway to the gate, his legs began to hurt, but he was used to that, so he kept running. He looked over his shoulder once to see if anyone was chasing him. He saw no one. He ran on. He looked back again, and this time he ran smack into the gate. He bounced back from it and fell to the ground.

He was glad there was no one around to see him, for he felt foolish. If anyone had seen him crash into the gate, he would have wanted to kill that person. It would be terrible to have someone around who had seen him do such a foolish thing. It would be horribly embarrassing. But there was no one. He crawled to the gate and pulled himself to his feet. He tried to open the gate. Once it was open, he would be free. He pulled on the gate. It did not open. He rattled it back and forth, and still it did not open. Then he saw the big padlock and chain. He could not open it. It was locked firm. He started to cry. He turned around and leaned back on the gate and allowed himself to slide down to a sitting position. He sat there and cried, leaning back against the hated gate. His legs hurt.

He had only wanted to get out so he could go home and see his mother. He had not seen her for a very long time. He wanted—suddenly, it came back into his mind: his mother was dead. His tears began to flood his cheeks. His mother had always been so good to him. She had taught him school at home, had taught him his numbers, and then she had gotten him his first job—really the only job he had ever had—working for old Walker in his store. He had worked there for three years. He remembered it well. And then the man had lost his stores and had not been able to pay Wil. He had given him some law books, and Wil had done well with them. And his mother had sold some land and given Wil the money to open his own store. He had done so well that he soon owned seven stores and fifty slaves; he had become a wealthy man.

Why did she have to die? He cried for a while longer. So she would not be there at his home at Stekoih. Sarah would be there, though, and he loved Sarah with all of his being. He wanted to see Sarah. She would love him and take care of him. Oh, God, his legs hurt. He stretched them out straight in front of him there on the ground. They still hurt. He wanted to scream out, but he decided against it. Screaming might attract some unwanted attention.

He wished that he had his knife or his sword. He might be able to break the chain or the lock. But then, he might just break the blade. He wished that he had one of his pistols. He could shoot the lock or the chain and break them that way. Of course, the shot would rouse the guards, but he could swing the gate open and run like hell from them. Oh, hell, his legs hurt. In addition, he was starting to hear the roaring sound in his ears again. He considered getting up and going back to his cell, but he did not move. Instead, he just sat there, leaning back on the hated gate, and tried to relax.

The weather was pleasant, just a bit cool in the dark night, and he could hear the sounds of the night bugs. He had always found their sounds soothing, since his early days at Mount Prospect, or more accurately, Raccoon Creek. He loved the bugs for the sounds they made at night. He toyed with the idea of getting up and climbing the fence, but he wondered if he was too old for that. He wondered just how old he was. He wished that Cudjo would come by to visit him. Cudjo would know how old he was. How long had his mother been gone, he wondered, and he wished that he knew how his Sarah was doing. He loved her so. Why would she not come to visit him?

Soon he drifted off to sleep. His head nodded and fell back against the gate. His dreams came, and they were filled with Civil

War battles, arguments with congressmen, stickball games, land purchases, and other big things that had filled his life. His head dropped suddenly, unexpectedly, and he brought it back upright with a jerk. It woke him. He looked around, and he was bored. His was bored with this place, and he was bored with his life.

He felt something on his arms, and he looked down to see long black feathers that looked as if they grew out of his arms. He was astonished. He lifted his right arm until it stuck out straight from his side, and he saw the feathers clearly. He lifted his left arm and turned his head to the left. It was all true. Both his arms were well feathered.

He managed to stand, and then he raised both arms even higher and brought them down again. When he did that, he felt a slight lift to his body. He flapped his arms—or his wings—more, harder, and at the same time, he bent his knees slightly and then shoved off as hard as he could. He was going up—up into the sky. He flapped his wings and rose higher and higher. It was wonderful. He had never before felt the breeze this way.

It was a cool and refreshing breeze. He rose higher into the sky, and he looked down and all around. Never before had he seen such a sight. He felt like he could see everything. He was higher than the highest mountaintops. The wretched place where he was held prisoner looked strange to him from up there. He searched around until he found his own house there in Stekoih. He had flown quite a distance already. He spread his wings wide and then held them still. He was floating along like the wide, white clouds he drifted through.

He did not even need to flap his wings anymore, just stretch them out and glide along. It was so peaceful. Why, he wondered and asked himself, had he waited so many years to do this? He could go anywhere around the world and see anything—everything. Then the feathers were gone, almost as quickly as they had appeared. He hovered there in the clouds for an instant, and then he was falling faster and faster.

The next thing he knew someone was shaking him by the shoulders. He jerked his head when he came awake. He looked at the strange man standing there before him, leaning over him with his hands on Wil's shoulders. The man looked vaguely familiar, and his face wore a look of concern.

"Mr. Thomas," the man said. "Mr. Thomas, what are you doing out here? Have you been here all night? We were worried about you, Mr. Thomas."

"Why?" said Wil. "Why should you be worried? I'm perfectly all right. I just came outside for some fresh air. That's all. And I wanted to listen to the bugs."

"To the bugs?" said the man, and Wil thought that the question sounded as if the man actually thought that he was crazy. Well, he was, of course. Absolutely batty. Nutty as a fruit cake. Mad as a hatter. He looked deeply, searchingly into the man's eyes.

"Do you think that I'm mad?" he said.

"Oh, no, sir. You're ill is all. Come along with me. We'll make you well."

"I'm not ill at all. I feel perfectly all right," said Wil, but he allowed the young man to help him to his feet. His legs were no longer hurting him, and the roaring had left his ears. "Who are you?" he said to the young man. "You're George, aren't you?"

"Yes sir. I'm George. Now let me take you back to your room."

"Yes. Of course."

George held onto Wil's right arm as they started walking to the main door at the front of the building. It was a straight walk along a sidewalk. As they moved along, Wil lifted his head to look at the clouds in the sky. They were not rain clouds. They were white and puffy, pretty clouds dotting a beautiful blue sky. Wil thought that the world looked perfectly fine and healthy. There could be nothing wrong anywhere. "I'm not ill, George," he said.

"Well, but you'll be more comfortable in your room, sir. You were just sitting on the ground and leaning back against a wire fence. That can't have been comfortable. Won't you feel better in your bed?"

"I suppose so. Take me there."

"That's where we're going, Mr. Thomas. We'll be there soon now."

They reached the main door, and George pulled it open and guided Wil through. He let the door shut itself behind them as he walked Wil through the big main room. Then they turned down the long hallway. Wil studied the hallway as they ventured down it. All the doors in a row. The dim light. "Where are we?" he said.

"We're almost to your room, Mr. Thomas," said George. "Just three more doors is all. Now, here we are."

George opened the door to Wil's room and guided him through. Wil stopped and stared. He studied the room, every detail. "Ah," he said at last, "my cell."

"Here," said George, "let me help you out of your coat."

"I don't want out of it," said Wil. "I'm perfectly comfortable in my coat."

"All right then. Do you want to lie down on your bed?"

"No. I don't. I want to sit in that chair."

"Very well." George led Wil to the chair and helped him to sit. "Are you all right now?"

"I have been all right. You keep making out like I'm sick. I'm all right. I want some coffee."

"I'll fetch you some," said George. "Just sit here and wait. I'll be right back." George rushed out of the room. Wil looked around. Everything looked familiar, but then, nothing looked familiar. In another moment, George returned to the room carrying a cup and a carafe.

"Who are you?" said Wil.

"It's George, sir."

"Are you mad, too?"

"Uh, no sir. I don't believe I'm mad."

"Then what are you doing here, in this place?"

"I work here, sir."

"Oh, I see. Is that my coffee?"

"Yes, sir. I've brought your coffee. Here. I'll pour you a cup."

"Thank you."

Wil took the cup and sipped from it. "Ah," he said, "that's very good."

"Thank you, sir. Will you be all right now?"

"I'm perfectly all right, except I'm too warm. Why do I have on this heavy coat?"

"Let me help you off with it."

Wil stood up and George slipped the coat off his shoulders and carried it to the closet to hang it up. "Is that better, sir?"

"Much. Thank you."

"Well, I'll be going now, sir, unless there's something else you require."

"Go on," said Wil. "Get on with you."

George left the room, shutting the door behind himself, and Wil's eyes began to tear again. "Mother," he said. "Mother, where are you?" He stood up and rushed to the door, flinging it open. He thrust his head out into the hallway and looked in both directions. He stepped out and stood in the middle of the hall, turning around and around, looking. He saw no one in the hall. "I thought my mother was out here," he said, as if he were explaining his behavior to someone. But there was no one there. "Oh, yes," he said. "I believe she's dead." He walked back into his room and to the chair and sat back down. He picked up his cup and took another sip.

He looked around the room until he found himself in the mirror on the far wall. He stared at himself there for a moment or two, and then he said, "I'm so old now, I guess everyone I know is dead."

CHAPTER ELEVEN

Narrow Escapes

Colonel William Holland Thomas had recruited a number of engineers, masons, carpenters, and blacksmiths, all of whom would be used to repair bridges and anything else that had been damaged by the Yankees. They would not do any fighting. These men were east Tennesseans who did not want to fight in the war. But then Thomas's legion had been put under the command of General Alfred E. Jackson, an energetic old fussbudget, who immediately ordered Thomas's engineers to lay aside their tools and pick up weapons. There were a bunch of parolees, as well, captured Confederates who had been released by the Yankees on the condition that the men promise not to fight anymore. Jackson had ordered them back into battle.

Colonel Thomas, disregarding the difference in rank, berated the general. "I shall write a letter to President Davis, my cousin, telling him how you have made a liar of me and of these men, these parolees. That is not a gentlemanly thing for you to do, General. I believe the president will see things my way."

General Jackson, his face flushed with anger, called out to a subordinate, "Arrest Colonel Thomas for disobedience of orders," he shouted. Thomas was scheduled for a court-martial, but then Burnside's Yankee forces swept into Knoxville, capturing it for the Union and putting the Confederate command there into disarray. The court-martial proceedings never took place. The next time, Thomas was not so lucky.

In 1864, desertions from the Confederate Army in western North Carolina were common. From time to time, some of those deserters returned to Colonel Thomas wanting to return to the Army. Thomas wrote to the War Department asking permission to accept them back into the ranks, but he was refused permission to do so. He accepted them anyway. Colonel John B. Palmer was given command over the western district of North Carolina, and Palmer and Thomas did not agree on much of anything. Thomas refused to obey Palmer's orders. He was arrested and taken to Goldsboro, North Carolina, for trial.

Colonel Thomas was charged with "knowingly entertaining and receiving deserters into his command," of "conduct unbecoming to an officer and a gentleman," of "conduct prejudicial to good order and discipline," and of "incompetency and disobedience of orders." Thomas stood before the board and declared himself, "Not guilty."

Thomas spoke in his own defense. "When Colonel Walker, sick in his bed, was attacked and murdered by Union-sympathizing bushwhackers, I realized the need to protect the good people of western North Carolina above the need to obey orders," he said. "My superiors did not always recognize that great need. Much that I did was done out of the desire to pacify the Union-sympathizing citizens of western North Carolina and eastern Tennessee." One of his lieutenants testified that Thomas often said that "good treatment would win over [the Unionists] but harsh treatment would drive them to the federal Army." Major Stringfield of the Thomas Legion said that often Thomas "acted with more wisdom than those over him."

However when the trial ended, Thomas was found guilty. He appealed the case to a higher court and boarded a train for Richmond. In President Jefferson Davis's office, Colonel

Thomas outlined to his cousin the charges that had been filed against him. He summarized the testimony at the trial both for and against himself, and he pled his case eloquently. When he was done, the president reversed the decision of the court-martial and fully exonerated Thomas, sending him back to his command.

And so, thought Wil Usdi, recalling these events, I triumphed once again, narrowly escaping disgrace. How could such a man be a madman? I have been a leader of men. I have secured land for my friends, the Cherokees, against insurmountable odds. I have been a senator for the people of western North Carolina and have gotten roads built for them and brought a railroad in. I have fearlessly led gallant troops for the Confederacy. All of these things I have done, and for what? To be forgotten and left to rot in a stinking cell, shunned as a madman. And then out loud he said, "How weary, stale, flat, and unprofitable seem to me all the uses of this world! Fie on't! ah, fie! 'tis an unweeded garden that grows to seed; things rank and gross in nature possess it merely."

I am quoting from *Hamlet,* he thought, and Hamlet, too, was a madman. Or was he mad? He may have been only pretending madness. The scholars all disagree on that point. They argue it endlessly. Was Hamlet mad or was he not? Is Wil Usdi mad or is he not? Perhaps, like Hamlet, I am but mad north-north-west. Perhaps. He suddenly rushed to the door to his cell and jerked it open. Leaning out into the hallway, he shouted, "George. George. I want you." Then he went back to his chair and sat down.

Then George, reliable George, appeared, opening the door.

"Mr. Thomas," he said, "what is it? What do you want?"

"I want my Sarah," said Wil. "Why has she not come to see me all these years, all these long years?"

George paused. His face took on a long appearance. He walked into the room near to Wil Usdi, and at last he said, "Mr. Thomas, I am sorry to have to tell you, once again, that Mrs. Thomas passed away about a year ago. The last time she came to see you, you did not know her. You looked her right in the face, close to her, and you said, 'Who are you?' She was terribly upset. She told you who she was, and you said it again. 'Who are you?' When she left, she was weeping. She died about a year ago, Mr. Thomas."

"What? No. It can't be. My Sarah? My wife? My love. My life. Oh, George, I cannot stand it. It is too much. George, is everyone I know dead?"

"Oh, no sir. I don't believe that they're all dead. But you are a very old man, Mr. Thomas, and many of your old friends have passed away, I'm sure. Your children are still alive and well, though, and some of your old friends are still with us."

"And enemies too, I imagine."

"I don't believe you have enemies, Mr. Thomas."

"Of course I have. Every great man has enemies. He cannot accomplish great things without making enemies. I'm sure they are all rejoicing because I'm locked away here in this cell."

"You're not in a cell. You can walk out of here anytime you like. You can go down to the lounge or to the dining room. You can even go outside. You're not locked in at all."

"But can I go out the gate? Can I go to my home? Can I go to Stekoih? To Cherokee?"

"You're ill, Mr. Thomas. We have to keep you here in this," he paused, "hospital for your own good."

"To cure me? Is there a cure for madness?" He looked at himself in the mirror for a long moment. Then he said, "George, I want coffee."

"I'll fetch you some right away."

"And bring an extra cup," said Wil, "for yourself. I want company."

George left the room and returned soon with a carafe and two cups. He poured one for Wil and one for himself, and he sat down on the edge of Wil's bed, facing Wil where he sat in his chair.

"Mr. Thomas," said George, after sipping his coffee, "how did you come to be so familiar with the Cherokees?"

"Ah," said Wil, "the Cherokees. The Cherokees are a great people. At an early age I went to work for a man with a trading post among them. Most of the people I worked with could speak no English. I had a young assistant, a Cherokee, who spoke both languages, and he taught me to speak the Cherokee language. And then I was adopted by a grand old man. Yonaguska was his name."

"What does that mean?"

"It means the drowning bear. Yonaguska. He called me an orphan, and he adopted me. Between my young clerk and my old adopted father, I learned a great deal. I learned to speak the language fluently. I attended ball plays and stomp dances. I hunted with them and fished with them. It was a glorious life. I had signed a contract with the store owner to work for three years for one hundred dollars; but at the end of the three years, he could not pay me. He was bankrupt and had to close his stores. He gave me a set of law books, and I studied them. So when the Cherokees had to face problems regarding their status in this state and their ownership of land, Yonaguska asked me to be their legal representative. I agreed, and I worked for them for years. I was very successful too, I may add."

"And then, I heard, you became their chief."

"What?"

"Is it true that you were their only white chief?"

"That is a falsehood based on a misunderstanding of my role with them. I was their legal advisor. I was their friend. Many people misinterpreted my role with them and called me their chief. No. It is not true."

George thought, the old man is very articulate. His memory is quite sharp for those early years of his life. Why could he not remember his own wife when he last saw her, and why did he not remember that she is dead? What kind of an illness has possessed his mind?

"My legs are starting to hurt," Wil said.

"Mr. Thomas," said George, "when you were so busy with the business of the Cherokees, why did you decide to run for the North Carolina Senate?"

"I was running around a great deal in those days," said Wil, "going to Washington on Cherokee business, and moving from one of my own stores to another. I realized that our roads were pathetic. The western part of our state was in great need of attention. I believed that we needed a railroad through here as well. I ran for office to see if I could get something done about those things."

"And from what I have heard, you accomplished those goals."

"I did indeed. And I voted for the establishment of a madhouse, and I voted for secession. Two dubious achievements seeing how things turned out."

"I recently heard something very strange, Mr. Thomas," said George. "I heard that after General Lee surrendered, you were forced to capture Waynesville from the Yankees before you could surrender. Is there any truth in that peculiar rumor?"

Wil smiled. "I'll tell you about that," he said. "You know,

Waynesville is like it's in the bottom of a bowl. It is surrounded by lofty mountains. Colonel Bartlett and Kirk the renegade had captured Waynesville for the Yankees. I had not yet heard the news of Lee's surrender, and I took my legion to the mountains surrounding Waynesville. I had the Cherokees build hundreds of fires on the mountain slopes so that it would appear to the Yankees in Waynesville that thousands of Confederates were gathering there. Then the Cherokees began to sing and dance. The Yankees, of course, had heard the story about the Cherokees scalping Yankee soldiers, so they became frightened.

"Colonel Bartlett sent out a flag of truce and asked for a conference. I went down with Colonel Love and twenty of the biggest, meanest-looking Cherokees I could gather. The Indians were stripped to the waist, painted, and decked out in feathers. They looked as ferocious as we could make them look. When we got into the town and were in the conference, I stood before them all and said loudly, 'I have my Cherokees all over those mountains around you. If you do not surrender, I will turn my Indians loose on you and you will all lose your scalps.' Well, someone came in with the news of Lee's surrender, and that changed the complexion of things. As it turned out, we surrendered, but the terms were very favorable to us."

"But I've heard that the last shot of the war took place there," said George.

"It did indeed. At least it was the last shot of the war in the east, certainly in North Carolina. It was before the incidents I have just described to you. I had heard that Bartlett was in Waynesville, and I sent Lieutenant Robert Conley, a fine soldier and the head of Conley's Sharpshooters, to circle the town and find out if it was true. Conley moved his Sharpshooters through some woods down near the town and ran right into Bartlett's troops. A brief battle followed in which Conley shot and killed a Yankee. The rest fled. And that was the last shot."

George finished his cup of coffee and said that he must report back to work. He refilled Wil's cup and left the room. Wil Usdi sat reminiscing about the war, thinking about the gallantry of young Conley, the man said to be the first in and the last out of any battle. The best damn rifle shot that Wil had ever seen. Yes, if Lee had not surrendered, the Thomas Legion would surely have captured Waynesville. The war might have ended very differently. But what the hell? Damn. His legs were now hurting him badly and his ears were roaring.

He wondered what was happening with his stores. Why did no one tell him what was going on with his stores? He thought that his son Willie, or William Holland Thomas, Jr., was taking care of them, but he wasn't at all sure that Willie was up to the chore. Willie would probably make a mess of things. Of course, the war had already made a mess of Wil's business, but he did not think that Willie, as young as he was, was capable of running a business. How old was Willie? Twenty-three? Or twelve? Of course, Wil had run a store when he was but twelve, or was it thirteen? He wasn't at all sure.

Surely someone should inform him of the state of his own businesses. Someone should keep him posted on the affairs of his own life. Damn them all. Damn his own family for neglecting him the way they were. Then unexpectedly, later that same day, or was it a different day, Wil couldn't be certain, George reappeared to inform him that Mr. Mooney had come back for another visit. Wil's spirits were revived immediately. "Show him in right away," he demanded. Mooney came into the room looking like he was ready for a cabinet meeting with Washington officials.

"Osiyo, Wil Usdi," Mooney said. "I trust I am finding you in good spirits."

"Never better, Mr. Mooney," said Wil. "Please sit down. Would you like some coffee? I'm afraid I only have one cup. I'll call for another."

"Never mind, Wil Usdi. I have had quite enough coffee already today. I have come to ask you if you can tell me some things about the Cherokee involvement in the late war."

"Of course I can," said Wil, and he went on in great detail, telling all the things he had just told to George and more, much more. Mooney took profuse notes, and the interview lasted for at least two hours. When it was over, Wil's mood changed again. He was somber and depressed. He was alone again, and that was the thing that depressed him most—being alone.

He tried to recall something pleasant in his life, and the thing that came to his mind was being alone in the back room of his first store with one of his women. He wasn't at all sure who it was, but he recalled her features, the smoothness of her skin and the roundness of her breasts and buttocks. He remembered the feel of her as his hands roved over her lovely body, and it was a wonderful time. It was as if it had just happened. It might have been sixty years ago, but it could have been only minutes.

CHAPTER TWELVE

Wandering in the Desert

George came into Wil Usdi's cell with a breakfast tray. He walked across the room and placed the tray on the table. "Get out of here, and take that damn mess with you," said Wil.

"Oh, Mr. Thomas," said George, "it's just your usual breakfast. That's all."

"I don't want that shit. It tastes like cardboard. Get it out of here."

"I have to leave you your breakfast," said George. "I'll just leave it here. Maybe you'll change your mind in a little while."

George turned to leave the room. Wil slid his fingers under the edge of the tray and suddenly flipped the tray over flinging it and all its contents onto the floor, making a terrible racket and a horrible mess on the floor. George spun around frightened.

"Mr. Thomas," he said in an excited voice. "Why did you do that?"

He moved as if to clean up the mess, but Wil shouted at him again, "Get out of here. Get out. Get out."

George rushed out of the room, slamming the door behind him. Wil stared at the far wall, his expression stern. He thought about the breakfasts his mother used to prepare for him, and later the ones that his lovely Sarah had prepared. Oh, they were good. They were delicious. Why could not Mother or Sarah come here and fix a meal for him? What would be wrong with that? It wouldn't hurt anything. He would love to have a fine breakfast like the ones he used to get at home.

The cooks at this loony bin were atrocious. He wondered where they got them, where they came from. From jails? From other loony bins? Perhaps they just picked them up on the street. They were damn sure not professionals. Was there not a school somewhere for cooks? Why could they not recruit their cooks from that school? That would be good. He would have to make that suggestion to whoever was in charge of hiring around this madhouse.

His door came open and two attendants came walking in. He did not know them. They were both big and mean looking, and their expressions were serious. "Who are you?" Wil said. One of them said, "Come along with us, Mr. Thomas." Wil stood up and braced himself for a fight. He backed up to the far wall. He glanced hurriedly around the room, hoping to spot his sword. He would like to slash at these two arrogant bastards. Then they had a hold of his arms, and they were dragging him along. "Let go of me," he shouted. "Unhand me, villains. Get out of my room. Leave me alone."

The next thing he knew, he was chained to a brick wall. His shirt had been stripped off, so he tried not to lean on the wall, because the bricks were cold to his bare chest and belly. "Where am I?" he shouted. "What's going on here?" One of the two brutes who had dragged him from his cell walked up close and spoke into his ear. "Mr. Thomas," the man said, "you're in the therapy room. You've behaved very badly, and your behavior must be corrected. It's all for your own good."

The man walked away, and Wil twisted his head trying to see what was behind him. He saw the two men, and each was holding a long, slender, flexible cane pole in his right hand. "What are you doing?" Wil shouted. Then he heard a swish that was followed by a sharp pain across his bare back. "Ow," he yelled. "Oh, stop that. I'm not a slave. I'm a free man. You can't do this to me." There was another swish and another stripe across his back. "Ahhh, ah, you're torturing me. Stop it." Then the swishing and the painful stripes continued with regularity. Tears began running from Wil's eyes. "I'll kill you," he said, mumbling. "I'll kill both of you. And I'll scalp your carcasses after you're dead." Swish. He screamed.

He was still screaming and cursing, but the whipping seemed to have stopped. He stopped screaming. He was quiet, trying to figure out what had happened, where he was. He tried to move his arms but found that he could not. He looked down to see that he was dressed in a heavy, white canvas kind of a thing. It had long arms, and his own arms had been crossed over his chest. The long arms of the damned shirt seemed to have been tied behind his back. A straitjacket, that's what it was. A chemise for lunatics. He was sitting on a floor in a pile of straw. He struggled to get his feet under him and to stand up. At last he managed to do it, but his legs hurt.

He turned around and around looking, and he discovered that he was in a very small cell. The walls were brick. There was nothing in the cell but the straw on the floor and a bucket in a corner. He walked over to look in the bucket, but it was empty. He decided that he knew what it was for, but he couldn't for the life of him figure out how they thought he would manage to use it, trussed up the way he was. His mouth was dry, horribly dry. He walked to the door. It was a solid door. No window. Not even a peephole.

"George," he shouted. "George, where are you?"

There was no answer. He shouted again. This time it was, "Anyone. Anyone out there." The shouting made his dry mouth worse. He wanted a drink of water. That wasn't so much for a man to ask for, even a madman. "Water," he shouted. "I need water." No one answered. No one came around. He was alone. Absolutely alone. His legs hurt, and now the roaring started in his ears again. As if that weren't bad enough, he began to feel the pain on his back from where he had been whipped. Oh, God, he was miserable. He looked up at the ceiling, and he cried out, "What have I done to deserve this?"

He sat down on the straw and leaned back against the wall. He did not feel the cold of the bricks because of the thickness of the material from which the straitjacket was made. He closed his eyes, and he looked at the endless sand ahead of him. The dunes rolled along one after the other. The wind blew, a hot, dry wind, and it blew sand in his face. It got in his eyes and in his mouth, and it made his thirst almost unbearable. There had to be water somewhere, and so he was walking. With each step, he sank into the loose, hot sand, and sand slipped into his shoes and filled them, and it hurt his feet when he walked. He thought about taking them off to pour the sand out, but he could not move his arms.

He continued walking, or trying to walk, through the fine sand, which seemed to be the entire world just now. It was like trying to walk in running water. He hated the sand. And from above, the hot sun was beating down. He could feel it burning his skin. He laughed a little at the thought that much more of this would make him look like an Indian. Wouldn't that be ironic? Chief Wil Usdi? He walked for what seemed like days. He couldn't recall any nights, though. It was always daytime with the sun beating down on him.

And then suddenly it was all gone. The sand, the hot sun. He was lying on straw in the small dark cell with its brick walls and its single bucket in a corner. He struggled to his feet, and his legs hurt. There was that roaring in his ears. He finally managed to get to his feet, and he staggered to the door. There was no opening, not even a slit in the door. Still he thought he would try. He screamed at the top of his voice.

"Water. I want water. Someone bring me a drink of water. I'm dying of thirst in here. Someone. Anyone. Bring me water."

When his extreme thirst combined with screaming really dried out his throat, he stopped the screaming. No one could hear him. Or else, they were content to let him die of thirst alone in the tiny cell. He hated them. He would like to kill them. He staggered back to his new bed of straw and attempted to sit down, but he fell. Then he stretched out and began to whimper, and he spoke in a small voice. "Water. Water. I want water."

Slowly he drifted into a kind of sleep, but it was really a dream, a nightmare. He was in a small boat, and he was being tossed by great waves. He looked around, and he could see nothing but water, rolling, tossing in waves that looked like they could sweep houses away. There was no land in sight. He turned around, looking in all directions. He realized in a moment of extreme horror that he was alone on the ocean, in the middle of the ocean. There was plenty of water, but it was ocean water, salt water.

> Water, water, everywhere,
> And all the boards did shrink;
> Water, water, everywhere,
> Nor any drop to drink.

It was terrible. It was ghastly. There was nothing he could do. He was at the mercy of the elements, and as far as he knew, the elements had no mercy. He thought about calling on God, but at just that moment, he was not at all sure of the existence of God. What God would place him in a tiny boat, alone in the middle of the ocean? With water everywhere and not a drop to drink? "God damn God," he said out loud. And that blasphemy frightened him.

What would God say to him or do to him for that bit of blasphemy? He shuddered to think about it. Perhaps some other little bit of blasphemy from his past was the cause of his present circumstances. It was dangerous to blaspheme God. He was a fool. "I myself am the cause of all my miseries," he said. "No one else is to blame. Mother did her best. She raised me right. Reading the Bible. Saying my prayers. That's it. That's it. I need to pray." He struggled to get up onto his knees, and he wished that he could fold his hands, but he could not. His arms were firmly lashed to his body.

On his knees, he leaned his head back and looked toward the heavens. "Lord God Above All," he said, "this is Wil Usdi, your faithful servant calling to you. God, I am in desperate need of your help. I've been imprisoned here in this horrible cell by my enemies, who think that I am a madman, a lunatic. I do not believe that I am a lunatic. I beg you to deliver me from this, my torture. Please save me, Lord. I need a drink of water."

He waited for a response. There was nothing. No voice. No sound. No vision. No one brought him water. He was devastatingly disappointed. God had ignored his plea. God did not care about him or, perhaps, did not exist. He did not like to think about either of those possibilities, but he could not help himself. One of the two had to be true. There was no other possible explanation.

He fell back onto his bed of straw and began to weep uncontrollably. It was a hard lesson he had just learned and an unpleasant one. He no longer had any family or friends, and now, with no God, he was absolutely alone in the cruel world. Alone. One small, weak, old man. Alone. He did not even have anyone to talk to. His family did not visit him, and it made him furious. It also made him sad, unbearably sad. What was he supposed to do? He had no idea, and there was no one with whom he could talk about it. He wanted Sarah. He wanted her desperately. He was madly, uncontrollably in love with her. He wanted to hold her in his arms.

He would not even need to talk to her or hear her speech, if he could only hold her. He missed her more than he could put into words, more than he could ever tell anyone. The one thing he hated the most about his recent discovery that there was no God, was that he could not go to heaven and find Sarah waiting there for him. He would never see her again.

Oh, he would like to stroke her hair, smell her body lying close to his, touch her all over, and feel her tender breasts. Oh, God, he could not allow himself to fall into such thoughts. They were too maddening, and he was already a madman. Madman! Lunatic! How could he stand it? How could he hold on? What could he hold on to?

CHAPTER THIRTEEN

Tsali

They returned him to his room after a few days. How many days was it? He did not know. It seemed to him that he had lain on that smelly straw for weeks, months even. It may have been only two or four days; he did not know. He knew only that of all things, he was happy to be back in his own cell. He spent hours looking around, checking through the closet and searching through all the drawers. He wanted to make sure that all his things were where he had left them. He could not determine that anything was missing. He could not, of course, find either his gun or his knife. His sword was nowhere to be found either. But then, he had never found those things in this cell. The floor had been cleaned.

He realized that he was terribly hungry and he was still thirsty. Perhaps part of his treatment had been to starve him and to bring him well-nigh to death by thirst. His legs still hurt, and the roaring was still in his ears. He wondered if he should call out for George, or if calling out would make them believe that he was still mad. He decided to suffer in silence. But soon George actually opened the door and poked his head into the room.

"George?" said Wil Usdi.

"Mr. Thomas," said George, "it's good to have you back. Are you all right?"

"I'm terribly hungry, George, and I feel as if I'm about to die of thirst."

"I'm not surprised," George said. "They don't give you any food or water in that place where you were. I'll get you something right away if you like."

"I would like that very much, George."

George returned very quickly with a glass and a carafe of water and placed them on Wil's table. "I'll be back in two shakes with some food," he said.

"Thank you, George," said Wil.

While George was gone, Wil drank almost all of the water. He drank the first glass down without a break, not even to catch a breath. He drank the second glass a bit more slowly, but not by much. After that, he drank with a bit more leisure. He felt much better after the water. The desert was way behind him. His memory of it was fading fast. Even the vast ocean was fading out of his conscious mind. He was sipping water when George returned with the food tray.

"I hope this will be all right for you, Mr. Thomas," George said as he placed the tray on the table. He stepped back cautiously, as if he was afraid of what Wil might do with the tray. "Thank you, George," said Wil, as he picked up the spoon and began digging into something on the plate. He did not know what it was, but he dug a bite out of it and put the food into his mouth. He chewed it up and swallowed it down, before he began to think about it. Was it good? Was it awful? He decided that it was the best-tasting cardboard he had ever eaten.

"It's very good, George," he said. "Thank you."

George slipped quietly out of the room, leaving Wil to finish his meal alone and in peace. And Wil did that. He actually enjoyed the meal. He had been much nearer starvation than he even realized. He ate all of the food, all of which tasted the same, but he did not mind that for a change. It occurred to him that if the food turned awful on him again, all he needed to do was starve himself for a few days and then he would like it again. He finished the meal and sat for a few minutes alone in the cell, staring at the walls. George came back to get the tray.

"Is there anything else you'll be wanting, Mr. Thomas?" he asked.

"Thank you. No, George," said Wil.

"Mr. Thomas," said George, "that Mr. Mooney is back to see you. Shall I bring him in?"

"Mr. Mooney?" said Wil, his spirits suddenly rising. He stood up, and then he realized that he had not changed his clothes since they had brought him back to his private cell. "Mr. Mooney. Yes. No. Wait a few minutes so that I can change my clothes. Then bring him in along with two cups and some coffee. Please."

"Yes, sir, Mr. Thomas."

When George left, Wil quickly ripped off all his old clothes and tossed them onto the floor of the closet. He found clean trousers, a clean white shirt, and a nice enough jacket. He put them on, along with a clean pair of socks, and then he slipped his shoes back on. He did not feel any sand in them. He tied on a black tie and studied himself in the mirror. Just then his door opened and George popped his head in again.

"Are you ready, Mr. Thomas?"

"Ready, George."

George put the coffee and cups on the table and went back to the door. "Please come in, Mr. Mooney."

Mooney stepped into the room. "'Siyo, Wil Usdi."

"'Siyo, Mr. Mooney. I am very glad to see you again. I hope you are well and your work is continuing in good fashion."

"Thank you, Wil Usdi," said Mooney. "I am well enough, and

the work is progressing well. But I have come to ask more help of you."

"Oh?" said Wil. "What may I help you with?"

"I've been working on the Removal period, and I have heard stories about a man named Tsali, whom the whites call Charley. I've been told that you have some firsthand information on the subject."

"I have indeed."

"Could you enlighten me on the matter?"

"Please sit down, Mr. Mooney, and have a cup of coffee."

Mooney sat and Wil poured two cups of coffee. He then sat in his chair and took a sip of coffee. "Mr. Mooney," he said, "it was in 1838, I believe, and Tsali and his family had been taken from their cabin home. They were being marched down the mountain to the nearest of the holding places, the stockades, you know. They say that Tsali's wife was mistreated by one of the soldiers, and that was more than Tsali could take. He killed the soldier. Then he and his family ran away into the mountains. They found where several hundred other Indians were hiding out.

"General Scott was furious when he heard the news. He had almost completed the Removal, and it irked him to have this thing happen at this particular time. He said if those other Cherokees in the mountains would turn the killers in, he would ignore the rest of them. When this word reached the Cherokees, they agreed; and when it reached Tsali, he said that he did not want his own people hunting him down. He would turn himself in. He did so, and General Scott had some of the Cherokees to form a firing squad and shoot Tsali and his sons, all but the youngest. And so they did. Tsali sacrificed himself so that the rest might stay in their homeland."

"But isn't there more to the story than that?" said Mooney.

"Weren't you directly involved in some way?"

"I had some clients," said Wil, "who had reservations from the 1817 treaty. They had a right to stay in North Carolina. But when I heard about Tsali, I was afraid that the Army might round up all of them for removal. General Scott enlisted my help in tracking down Tsali. He offered me a fine sum of money for my aid, but I refused it for fear of what might be thought and said of me if I accepted it. Then I sought out Euchella and some of his followers, and we went in search of Tsali.

"I had explained to Euchella that if he and his followers would help me to run down Tsali, then his chances of remaining in North Carolina would be greatly improved. We were joined in Quallatown by Flying Squirrel and some of his men. In all there were perhaps sixty Cherokees and myself. After several days of marching through the woods, we came upon the fugitives, and they surrendered without incident. Then the officer in charge of the soldiers that were accompanying us held a quick trial and condemned the men. He then formed a firing squad of the Cherokees, and they shot Tsali and his sons. That's all I know of the incident. I hope that helps you, Mr. Mooney."

"It does indeed, Wil Usdi," said Mooney, still jotting his notes. "And from that point onward, the whites in the western part of the state seemed little concerned with the Cherokees who were not removed. Would you say that is correct?"

"I believe it is correct," said Wil. "They were too few to worry about, and the land they were living on was too poor to be of any interest to whites."

"That was land that you yourself had purchased for them, was it not?"

"It was, but before you think bad of me for purchasing poor land, let me say that what is poor land to a white man may not be so poor for a Cherokee."

"I think I understand," said Mooney. "Now, since those days, Tsali has become something of a folk hero."

"And rightly so," said Wil. "His sacrifice saved the homes of those Cherokees who stayed to form the Eastern Band of Cherokees. At that time, there were perhaps a thousand of them. Tsali is indeed a heroic figure to them."

"Thank you very much for your information on that important incident," said Mooney, "and now, if I may, I would like to jump ahead nearly thirty years. I understand that you were court-martialed during the Civil War, in September of 1864."

Thomas drew himself up smartly, almost as if at attention, but he remained seated. "That is correct, sir," he said. "I was accused of refusing to obey orders to punish deserters who returned to their duties. I was taken to Goldsboro for trial. In court, I pled not guilty. In spite of a great deal of support from my own officers and other officers of the Confederacy, I was found guilty. So I took a train ride to Richmond to see my cousin, the president, Jeff Davis. President Davis, of course, saw me. I explained the charges against me and the way the court proceedings had gone. Of course, I told him the outcome of the trial. The president reversed the whole matter, and I was fully exonerated.

"I always had my loyal supporters, Mr. Mooney. Back in 1864, I believe it was, fifteen of my good Cherokee soldiers had been captured. Yankee officers called them together and made the following offer. They would be released and be given five thousand dollars in gold if they would bring in my scalp. They conferred and then agreed, and were released. Afterward, they were remained busy during the war, hunting Yankee scalps."

Mooney chuckled at that tale and made some more notes. Following some more pleasant conversation, Mooney took his leave. For some time afterward, Wil Usdi felt remarkably good. He felt lucid and sane.

On his way out of the building, Mooney, on a whim, turned down the hallway toward the director's office. He had met with the director before, and they'd had a satisfactory visit. He was admitted quickly into the director's office. After the exchange of a few pleasantries, Mooney said, "As I'm sure you've guessed, I just came from a visit with Mr. William Thomas. I wanted to visit with you about his situation."

"Oh?" said the director.

"I believe Mr. Thomas to be recovered from whatever afflictions he has been suffering under all of this time. I found him to be pleasant, lucid, and quite alert."

"That's good news, Mr. Mooney."

"I hope that it's good enough news for you to consider releasing him under his own recognizance. I believe him to be perfectly capable of taking care of himself and his own business interests."

"Mr. Mooney, I will certainly take your recommendation under advisement."

It was a few days later when William Holland Thomas, Jr., received a letter from the mental institution at Morganton. The letter informed Willie that Mr. Thomas, Sr., was declared to be cured, and that Willie could pick him up at any time to take him home. Willie was elated. He told the rest of the household about the letter and arranged for a carriage right away. When the hospital received Willie's response to their letter and knew when to expect his arrival, George went to Wil Usdi's room to let him know.

"Mr. Thomas," he said, "you're being released."

Wil Usdi could not believe the news, could not trust his

senses. "Released?" he said, his voice betraying disbelief.

"Yes, sir," said George. "You've been declared sane. Your son is coming for you. He should arrive here tomorrow."

The next day, Wil's bags were packed and he was dressed in his best suit. He was so anxious for the arrival of his son that he was afraid that his anxiety would drive him back into madness. He paced the floor of his cell, back and forth, back and forth. He had been served breakfast and lunch and had eaten both meals. George had brought him a cup and a carafe of coffee, and he had a cup poured. He did not want to let his coffee get cold, so he stopped pacing now and then to take a sip. He was feeling wonderful.

All of this was over now, he thought. He would return to a normal life, his home, his stores, his Cherokee friends. Things would once again be as they had been in the past. Life was going to be great. When the knock finally came on his door, he was startled. The door opened and Willie stuck his head into the room.

"Papa?" he said.

Wil rushed to Willie to embrace him. "Willie," he said, "son."

"How good to see you, Papa, and what wonderful news."

Then old Cudjo stepped into the room behind Willie. "Mr. Thomas," he said, "you're looking just fine."

"Cudjo, my old faithful friend," said Wil. "I wasn't expecting you. It's wonderful to see you again."

Cudjo took Wil's bags out to the carriage, and Wil and Willie followed arm-in-arm. At the main front door, Wil said courteous good-byes to George and other of the staff and to the director. All wished him well, and he thanked them for all their help and care. Then the three men went out to the carriage together and climbed in. Cudjo took the reins, and the carriage rolled away from the building and headed toward home, Stekoih. Wil was in a glorious mood, and both Willie and Cudjo were obviously wonderfully happy.

As the carriage rolled along, Wil craned his neck this way and that, taking in the beautiful surroundings, thinking he had been deprived of the beauty of his native western North Carolina for far too long. He loved looking at the distant mountains, and the sight of the various greens on the mountainsides seemed to renew his soul. There was mist here and there on the mountains, looking sometimes like low-hanging clouds, other times like wisps of smoke rising to the heavens. It was all so glorious. Wil thought, it looks as if Jul'kala is sitting up there smoking his pipe.

But the ride was not all pleasant. They were not ten miles away from the hospital when Wil turned to his son and said, "Why didn't your mother come along? I was so anxious to see her." That was followed by an embarrassed pause, and then Willie said, stammering a bit, "Papa, she's dead now for some time. You knew."

"Oh, yes," said Wil. "Of course. I did know. I guess I had just forgotten for a moment."

The ride was silent after that, except, of course, for the clopping of the horses' hooves and the rattling of the carriage as its iron wheels bounced along the uneven road. When they passed a farmhouse, an occasional dog came running after them, barking. Huge crows would occasionally fly over, sounding their raucous caws. Wil was humiliated by his momentary lapse of memory, and both Willie and Cudjo were subdued by it as well.

I must be more careful, Wil told himself. I mustn't make any more such lapses. I have been cured. The hospital declared me to be. Willie and Cudjo must have their doubts now that I have slipped up so egregiously. My darling Sarah is long gone. How could I have forgotten it? It's almost unforgiveable. What else must I remember? Mother is gone. My slaves, including Cudjo, have all been freed. The war is over. I am no longer in the senate. Do I still have my stores? Do I still have my Cherokee clients? I must not say anything about anything that I do not recall for certain.

When they passed a familiar farmhouse, Wil mentioned the owner of the house. From then on, he made mention of where people lived or places where certain things had happened in the past. "Isn't that where old Tom Martin used to live?" he said.

"Yes, it is," said Willie.

"Do you recall, Cudjo, when I bought five hogs from him years back?"

"I sure do, Mr. Thomas."

"I think I paid him ten dollars."

"You did. Exactly ten dollars."

"And when we got them home, one of them ran away."

Cudjo laughed out loud. "Sure enough did. He was fast, too."

"We chased him all the rest of that day."

"I was plumb wore out from all that running."

"And we never saw him again, did we?"

"No, sir. We never did."

From then on, the rest of the trip was more relaxed. Each of three men had the same thought: perhaps everything will be all right after all.

CHAPTER FOURTEEN

The Lawsuit and More

Wil was all right at home at Stekoih for a little while, but then he went just a little crazy again, getting angry at something trivial and pushing Willie over a chair onto the floor. Cudjo was sent for the sheriff, and the sheriff was once again asked to return Wil to the hospital. "You mean the crazy house," Wil shouted. Willie, growing more than a little impatient, said, "Yes. The damned loony bin." Shortly thereafter Wil was back at home in his cell. He was well behaved. It was only a few days before he received a visit from his lawyer, whom Wil called Rance.

"It's hard for even me to believe, Wil," Rance said, "but the Cherokees have filed a lawsuit against you."

"I don't believe it," Wil said. "They wouldn't turn on me in that way."

"You remember that tract of land you bought for them adjacent to the original land you purchased for them along the Oconaluftee?"

"Yes," said Wil, "of course, I do."

Wil's memory was always excellent when it came to anything to do with the Cherokees.

"Well, it's been claimed that it is not theirs—that it is actually yours, instead—so your creditors are trying to get their hands on it."

"I bought it for the Cherokees."

"But you used your own money, and so your creditors are claiming that it is land you bought for yourself. The Cherokees are suing you because you called it your land, and therefore they are apt to lose it. They are suing you because you did not declare it to belong to them and make it safe for them."

"I could not. The state does not allow Indians to own land."

"But they say that you should have put it in the name of the corporation you founded for them."

"That land was purchased long before the corporation was set up. Once the corporation was in place, I just did not think of that piece of land. It was an oversight. Nothing more."

"I know that, Wil, and so do they, but apparently this is the only way they can keep the land safe for themselves. They must maintain that you defrauded them."

"I see."

"Now I can win this case for you, if I can show . . ."

"No," said Wil. "You must not. The Cherokees must win it. I always meant for the land to belong to them. We must not allow my creditors to get hold of it. I won't allow it."

"As your attorney, I must protest. Your finances are already in terrible shape. Should we lose this case it will just about ruin you."

"If I win this case, I will murder you. Do you understand me, Rance? I'll kill you and take your scalp."

Rance was at his most inept during the trial, and the Cherokees won the case. Their land was secured. Wil lost nothing except the land, as there was no monetary settlement. He was pleased with the outcome. Rance, on the other hand, was devastated. He felt like he had let his client down, and he was afraid that his own reputation would be ruined when the word got around. But Wil believed the Cherokees would be happy with the outcome, and that was really all that mattered—they had the land.

But then sitting alone in his cell for long hours, Wil brooded over the trial and the fact that his friends, the Cherokees to whom he had given so much of his life, had sued him, had accused him of defrauding them over a mere piece of land. It threw him into a deep depression. Might they try to kill him? He wondered. Had they turned against him? Did they, who had once loved him, now hate him? He longed for his long ago and dear friend Yonaguska. Yonaguska would set them straight if he were here.

A few more days crept by, and then Wil had a visitor from Qualla. He saw something vaguely familiar in the old Cherokee man's features, but he could not quite identify the man. The man put out his hand for Wil to shake, and then he said, "I was your clerk when you first went to work for Mr. Walker. I'm John."

Wil was terribly embarrassed that he had failed to recognize John. He pumped John's hand warmly. "It was you taught me to speak Cherokee," he said. "I'm so glad to see you. Welcome to my home." Then, with a little embarrassment in his voice, he added, "my cell." They made small talk for a little while.

"Wil Usdi," said John, his voice and his expression growing serious, "I came with some news."

"Yes? What news?"

"Wil Usdi, after the trial, some Cherokees came to believe that you truly did defraud us of some land. They said that you bought land for yourself with our money and that you resold some of our land to make money for yourself."

"How can they believe that of me?"

"I don't know," said John, "but they do. There are not too many of them, but they talk loud. They are persistent."

Wil stood and began pacing the floor; he had a very troubled look on his face. "Maybe if I went out there to talk to them. . . ."

"There's more, Wil."

Wil stopped his pacing and sat down. He looked at John intently.

"What more?"

"Some of them have asked a medicine man to conjure you because of what they believe you have done."

"Is he supposed to kill me? I would almost welcome it."

"No. Not kill you. He is supposed to make you lose your mind."

Wil burst into laughter. When at last the laughter subsided, he looked at John. "My friend," he said, "don't worry about that. Not a bit. You see, I've already gone mad. Years ago. They're too late." He laughed again. "Lose my mind, indeed. I'm as mad as a hatter."

"But Wil Usdi . . ."

"My dear and good friend," Wil said, "forget them. There is nothing they can do to me. No harm can come to me because of their conjuring. I am already well beyond their reach."

Alone in his cell that evening, Wil pondered his situation. How could they think that they could harm me? Did they not know that I am already in this prison for the totally insane and, in fact, was placed here long ago? I was locked away long before I even bought that land. If I have done wrong, I am already being punished for it. I have lost my dear mother. My wife, my love, has gone before me. My son no longer has any respect for me, much less any love. No one comes to visit me anymore. But how can they think that they can drive a madman mad? What foolishness. What clowns they must be.

He thought about the clowns he had seen in the circus years before. It was one of his times in Washington. It was before he was married. He was almost certain of that. A circus had come to town, and he went to see it—with a woman. He could not recall who the woman had been, whether she was a lover or just a friend. No. He believed that she was either a lover or a woman he was pursuing. She must have been a fine-looking woman, for he would never have let himself be seen out in public, even at a circus, with other than a fine-looking woman. They had gone to see the circus, and they had watched the clowns, who could not have been more foolish than these Cherokees who were now trying to cause him to lose his mind.

Wil began to feel guilty for thinking about a time he'd had with a woman other than his delightful Sarah. Sarah was his wife. More than that, Sarah was the love of his life. He adored her. She had been his whole life for years. There was never another like her. There could never be another. He loved Sarah with his whole being. She eclipsed the sun and the moon. His life before he met her had been a complete waste. He had started life anew when he met Sarah.

He tried to think more about the circus he had seen. There had been elephants and lions. And he and the woman he had been with delighted in seeing the monkeys in their cages. She had laughed and laughed, and later they'd had a grand time back in the hotel. Oh, no. He had to jerk his brain around to think of something else. Who was that woman? She had been a wonder and a joy to be with, both of them lying together in the hotel room bed, both of them stark naked. His brain was betraying him again. He had to make it stop. What was the matter with him? He was mad. That was it. He was mad for certain and for sure.

But she had been such a delight. How could it be possible to put her out of his mind? And after all, what was wrong in remembering? He wasn't hurting anyone by remembering past joys. No one had come to see him for quite some time, so if he thought of someone else, whose fault was it after all? There had been a number of women. He would try to recall them all. That would serve all the rest of them right. It was just what they deserved. He would think of all the women he had ever had as a form of revenge. But just then, George appeared in the doorway and announced a visitor, and in another minute, young Willie Thomas appeared.

"Hello, Pa," he said.

Wil looked at him, looked him right in the face and wrinkled his brow. "Who are you?" he asked.

"I'm Willie, Pa. You know me. I'm your son. I'm Willie."

Willie walked over closer to Wil, thinking that perhaps something was wrong with the old man's eyes. He got very close and looked his father directly in the eyes.

"Who are you?" said Wil.

Willie could feel tears welling up in his eyes, like they were behind his eyeballs, but soon they would work their way around. If he didn't get out soon, they would begin to run down his cheeks. He did not want the old man to see that, to see a stranger weeping there in front of him, for apparently that was what he had become, a stranger. "Never mind," he said. "I suppose I should be on my way. I guess I was looking for someone else." Willie turned abruptly and hurried out of the room. In the hallway he almost ran into George.

"Oh," he said, "excuse me."

"You're not leaving are you?" said George.

"Yes."

"That was an awfully quick visit."

"He doesn't even know me," said Willie. "I won't be back. If he doesn't know me, it doesn't do him any good, and it certainly doesn't do me any good. No, I won't be back."

Wil walked to his window and scowled out at the landscape. So someone did come to see me, he told himself, but I don't know him. It was a mistake. I don't want him for a visitor. Insipid little shit. How dare he come in here? If I had my sword, I'd have cut him. I would have. George opened the door and stepped in.

"Mr. Thomas?" he said.

"How dare you bring a stranger in here to my private room?"

"Mr. Thomas, that was your own son, Willie."

"Nonsense. I have no son. Wouldn't I know it if I had a son? Wouldn't I remember such a thing?"

"Well, sir, unless you were . . ."

George paused, an awkward pause for sure.

"Mad?" said Wil. "Unless I were mad? Is that what you wanted to say? Well, of course, I am mad, but that doesn't make that little fool my son. I never saw that person before in my life."

CHAPTER FIFTEEN

The Jailbreak

Colonel Thomas had been ordered to take his Cherokees to Gatlinburg to keep an eye on enemy movements. The Yankees had taken over Knoxville, Tennessee, and the Confederates were worried about all of eastern Tennessee and western North Carolina. While in Gatlinburg, Thomas sent out a few Cherokees on a scouting party to look for any enemy movements in the area. While they were out, a large Union Home Guard riding out of Sevierville overtook them and captured them. The Home Guard took their prisoners back to Sevierville and lodged them in the jail there.

When news of this reached Colonel Thomas, he went into a rage. He gathered up two hundred Cherokee soldiers and rode for Sevierville. The Union Home Guard was taken completely by surprise as the Cherokees swarmed into Sevierville, firing their guns and gobbling like wild turkeys. The Home Guard soldiers ran for their lives. Sixty of them threw down their arms and surrendered. Thomas demanded the keys to the jail, but none of the sixty captured men had them. They did not know where the keys might be. Thomas ordered the jail be broken into.

Two of the Cherokees shot the lock on the jail door, and they released the prisoners. They rode around the town and found six regular Union soldiers, whom they also captured. Then, with the sixty-six prisoners and all of their weapons, they headed back to Gatlinburg.

Almost immediately, the Federals responded by attacking Gatlinburg, anxious to recover their men and their captured weapons. As the Federals approached the town, Thomas's guards saw them and fired on them. The whole Rebel contingent was alerted. They formed a skirmish line and fired on the Yankees. But the Yankees outnumbered them and fought hard, wading a creek and climbing a hill into the Cherokee camp, where some of the Cherokees were busy preparing breakfast. They had to abandon that chore and go for their guns. On their way through the camp, the Yankees stopped long enough to grab corncakes out of the skillets and eat them. They then chased the Cherokees up the mountain through thick forest. Two Cherokees were slightly wounded. The Federals got some horses, muskets, and ammunition, and the Cherokees disappeared over the mountain. The Yankees could not keep pace with them on the heavily wooded mountainside.

Remembering all this, Wil said out loud to himself, "The most significant thing about the battle was that the bastards got my hat."

He stood up and wandered all over his room, opening drawers and rummaging through their contents. He threw things out of the closet and overturned boxes of papers. Where is my hat? He kept asking himself. Where is it? And my sword. Where is my sword? He wanted to put on his hat and wave his sword around in the air. "I am a Colonel in the Confederate Army," he shouted. Soon he wore himself out and went to the bed to lie down. "Why do I keep recalling the same stories?" he asked himself.

He found himself on the bank of a clear, running stream in the mountains near Raccoon Creek. Ahead of him water cascaded one hundred feet down to the creek. Wil was standing close enough to the falls that he could feel the thick spray from the water when it splashed on the rocks below. It was one of his favorite spots; it had been so for most of his life. The stream ahead, where the waters settled somewhat following their violent descent, was full of mountain trout. It was a peaceful spot, but not quiet, for the falling waters made a loud crashing and splashing sound that drowned out all other noises.

If he stayed still and quiet long enough, he might see deer come down to the stream for a cool, refreshing drink of water. Maybe a black bear would wade into the cold stream to fish, and now and then, with a little luck, Wil might see him catch one or two. A mist rose up from the base of the falls, and beyond that, one could often see a large rainbow of sparkling colors. Wil loved seeing the rainbow. It arched over the landscape like a giant, beautiful protector. Wil thought that nothing could attack his magnificent mountains while this lovely and strong guardian stood watch.

He loved the cooling shade of the many giant trees that lined the stream and grew above and beyond the falls, crawling up the mountain clear to the top. Their leaves rattled in a strong wind, and in lighter breezes, they would sway in unison. He loved picking and eating the berries that grew in the woods there.

Wil was a mountain boy, and he knew himself as such. He had been born to these mountains and had grown up with them and in them. He was a part of them and they of him. He knew that if anyone should forcibly remove him from these mountains, he would die.

He wanted to strip off his clothes and wade into the cold water, walk under the powerful shower of the mountain waterfall, feel the water beat on his body. He wanted to submerge himself in the stream and swim through it like the fish. He could not though. He could not even stand up to remove his clothes. Something was wrong, because what he was lying on did not feel like the ground. It was softer and smoother. He could not raise himself up. He could not even lift his arms.

He removed himself from the mountains with the power of his mind and imagined himself far away. He found himself in Washington once more, but then everything started spinning, and he woke up in his bed in the cell in the crazy house. He sat up and looked around. It had not worked. He was right where he had always been. Always been? He wondered. Perhaps he had never really been at Raccoon Creek. Never at the town of Cherokee. Never in the army. Perhaps he had always been in this room and the rest was delusion. Perhaps.

He could kill himself if only he could find his sword, or a knife even. He knew, though, that he could not find any such thing, so he did not bother getting up and going to look. If he had always been in this cell, how had he been born? Had he always been this wretched old man that he saw when he looked in his mirror? Always? Could he have been born this way? He could not imagine how that could have happened.

He had once read a book about something called vampires. They appeared to be human, but they were not. They lived for thousands of years. Once they had been human, but another vampire had bitten them and sucked out their blood, turning them into vampires. Could that have happened to him? And instead of a coffin, he was in this cell. He wondered if he could turn himself into a bat and fly out of the cell after the sun went down. He would enjoy flying around and biting people. God damn them all.

He would not need his sword or a knife if his teeth were sharp enough. He reached up slowly with his right hand, and with his fingers felt his teeth. They were not particularly sharp. If he could transform himself into a bat, the teeth would become sharper. He was sure of that. He thought and thought about it. He strained. He wasted several minutes at it, but nothing happened. He fell back down on the bed and tried to sleep.

He woke up on the back of a fast-running horse, and he had his sword! He was waving it around over his head, but there were hundreds of Yankees on horseback chasing him. He was not attacking. He was fleeing. He wondered where his legionnaires were. Perhaps they were up ahead waiting in ambush, and he was leading the unsuspecting Yankees into their hands. Soon the Yankees would all be dead and scalped.

But suddenly he was in the air. He had come out of the saddle, and he and the horse were both falling, falling, into nothingness. He lost his sword. He looked down, and he could see below him the frightened horse, his hooves flailing in the air. And far down below the horse, water, a river. They had gone over a cliff and were falling into a river. They seemed to fall forever, though, and the water never looked any nearer. He longed for the impact and the splash.

Then it came. A loud splash as the horse hit the water, and water splashed upward to smack him all over. He was still falling, but he hit the water a moment later, a long moment. He did not feel the impact, but he felt the intense cold as he sank into the icy water of the river, and he heard the loud splash. He was sinking down deep into the river. He was waving his arms around and kicking his legs in an attempt to move upward instead of down.

He did not like being down deep in the water. His arms and legs were getting tired, and his lungs seemed about to burst. Was this, he wondered, what his father had felt like just before he drowned a month or so before the birth of his only child?

He started making progress, moving upward toward the surface, and at last he struck it, and his head burst out of the water. His mouth opened wide to suck in great gulps of air. Just next to his head, something hit the water with a sound like "*spang*," and he looked up to see the Yankees far above on the ridge firing their weapons at him. He could hear the faint reports of the rifles, but mostly he saw and heard the balls hitting the water around him. As much as he hated to do it, he took a deep breath and went back down under the water, and he started to swim as fast as he could away from the Yankees up above.

Then he woke up again, and again he was in his bed and looking around at the walls of the cell. His clothes felt wet. At first he thought it was because of the river and the soaking he'd had. Then he realized it was all from sweat. He was angry. At what or at whom, he did not know, but he came up out of the bed fast and was standing on his feet on the floor. "Ahhh," he groaned out loud. His legs hurt, and then he heard the roaring in his ears. He clapped his hands to his ears trying to shut out the sound, but it was no use, for the sound was coming from inside his head, his insane head.

"I am a madman," he shouted at the top of his voice. "I am the maddest man in the country."

He thought about the Battle of—but why should he rehearse that again in his mind? He went over and over that battle. It seemed he could not remember anything else from the war. When his brain told him a story like the one he had just gone through, about being chased over the cliff by Yankees, it was pure fabrication. It had never really happened, and he knew that. Even in his madness, he could tell when his brain was making something up and when it was recalling something that had actually happened. "Maybe I am not the maddest man in the country," he said out loud, "but surely I am up there close to the top of the list."

Suddenly he felt all right again. The roaring was gone from his ears. His legs were no longer hurting him. He relaxed and lay back on his bed. He was comfortable. But he was bored. He asked himself what did he want out of this life? He was relatively successful. He had businesses. He had been a senator. He had been a colonel in the army. He had been a great legal advisor to an Indian tribe. What more could he want? Did he perhaps want to be governor of the state? He could run for that high office. He had won political offices before. Perhaps he could be governor. Or how about president of the United States?

He might even be able to accomplish that. Why not? He had in his possessions somewhere a letter from President Andrew Johnson granting him a pardon for all of his activities during the late war. And he had a hell of a good record of political activity. He might be able to make it that far. And why shouldn't he? Others with backgrounds as humble as his had done it, or nearly so. Look at what ol' Sam Houston had done. He had come out of a rural home and lived with Cherokees, just as Wil had done, and he had practically become a Cherokee. Then he had become a soldier, and later adjutant general of the state of Tennessee. From there he had become the governor of the state, and then he had gone to Texas where he had been general of the army, president of the country, and later governor of the state. What a record.

And he was certain that he had forgotten a few of old Sam's accomplishments.

And Wil could do those things, he told himself. Then he stood up and walked across the room to where the mirror hung on the wall. He looked at his image, and he was horrified to see the white hair, the wrinkled old face, and the sagging jaws. His hand went up to one cheek as if to check and make sure it was really his. "Who am I?" he said. "I can't accomplish those things. I'm way too old. How old am I?"

He ran to his door and flung it open. "George," he called out. "George, I need you."

In a couple of minutes George showed up. "What is it, Mr. Thomas? What's wrong? What do you need?"

Wil put his hands on George's shoulders and looked deep into George's eyes. His expression was pleading. "George," he said, "how old am I?"

"Why, Mr. Thomas, I can't remember exactly. I know that you're over eighty. Eighty-five or eight-six I think."

"That old?" said Wil. "Where have I been all that time?"

"Since the end of the war, I believe, you've been mostly right here. I think you were confined at Raleigh for a time, but you were transferred here as soon as this one was built. You've been mostly right here."

"All those years in a madhouse?" said Wil.

"Yes. You've been right here in this hospital."

"Call it what it is," Wil snapped. "A madhouse. That's what it is. A madhouse."

"Mr. Thomas, why don't you try to relax? You want to lie down on your bed and try to sleep?"

"I don't want to sleep. I'm not sleepy. I don't need any sleep.

I want to smoke, George. I have my pipe, but they won't let me keep tobacco here. I want to smoke."

"All right, Mr. Thomas. Let's walk outside. I can give you some tobacco. Come along with me."

Wil ran to his desk drawer and pulled it open. He took his pipe out of the drawer. "Let's go," he said. They walked out of his room arm in arm, down the hallway to the door that led outside. Once out in the yard, George dug into a pocket and brought out a tobacco pouch, which he handed to Wil. Wil filled the pipe bowl, and George struck a match and held it out. Wil stuck the pipe bowl under the flame and sucked. Soon, he had the pipe going. He drew deeply and exhaled long with a sigh. "This is good," he said. "You know, George, I've had this pipe for years, ever since it was given me by old Yonaguska himself. About the time he named me Wil Usdi. He was a fine old man was Yonaguska."

"And what did his name mean?" asked George.

"Drowning Bear," said Wil. "He was a fine man. I learned to speak Cherokee from him. And I learned many other things, too. He taught me almost everything I know. His grandson was our chaplain during the war. Unaguska was his name. He was a grand preacher. Even white men could sit and listen to him preach, and he didn't speak anything but Cherokee. Still, his sermons fascinated people who could not understand his words. Ah, George, those were the days."

"I imagine they were," George said. "I wasn't even born yet."

"No, you are a mere child."

"I must seem so to you, Sir."

Wil puffed at his pipe. "You're a fine boy, George.

"One fool reporter attended our church services and thought

that the Cherokee sounded like Hebrew," said Wil, and he started to laugh. "The damn fool had probably never even heard Hebrew spoken. He must have read what that idiot Adair wrote and been influenced by that. You know, Adair thought that the Cherokees were one of the lost tribes of Israel. Can you imagine?"

"It does sound far-fetched."

"Far-fetched? It's crazy. Adair belonged in a place like this. Not me."

CHAPTER SIXTEEN

The Madman Remembers History

"I'll tell you who really belonged in a madhouse, George," Wil said. "Old Chicken Snake, Andrew Jackson. The, by God, president of the United States. The very man who sent the Cherokee people to the West. That one. He was so mad that he thought he was a king. Did you know that? King Jackson the First, or King Andrew. Now there was a madman. He's dead, isn't he? I'm sure he's dead. And another one was that John Ross. The Principal Chief of the Cherokee Nation. He tried to stop me from collecting money for my Eastern Cherokees. But I got it anyhow. I got it in spite of him. He wanted to keep all of the Cherokee money for the Cherokee Nation way out West, leave nothing for these people out here. They deserved it. It was theirs, too. And I got it for them. Now there would have been a pair for you to have in this place. Jackson and Ross. And they hated each other.

"Governor Vance was another one. He blamed me that the Yankees captured his brother. It was not my fault, but the governor blamed me for it. He was crazy. And they've made him out to be such a hero to North Carolina. Bah. Fah. Phht. Governor Vance be damned. Perhaps he is. And that Abraham Lincoln, the one who started the war and freed the slaves, including my fifty, costing me and all other honest slave owners the money we had invested. Lincoln, the tyrant. He was a madman. But that good Southern boy and fine actor John Wilkes Booth took care of him, didn't he? They killed Booth for that, but he saved us all from any further actions of the madman Lincoln.

"And what about those hundreds of citizens of western North Carolina and citizens of east Tennessee who remained loyal to the Northern cause during the war? Their own neighbors and some of their own families were good Confederates, yet they were goddamned Tories. That damned deserter and traitor Kirk was one of the worst of them. When the war was over, they should have rounded up all of those Tories and put them in the madhouse. That's where they belonged. But, no, they put me in here instead. They called me the madman.

"Did I say that Kirk was the worst? Well, I was wrong. There was that Goldman Bryson. He was the worst. He was a devil. He led a gang of maybe 150 mounted robbers in the mountains of western North Carolina. They called themselves the First Tennessee National Guard. Balderdash. Our General Vaughan was ordered to locate the Guard and destroy it. He located it all right, but he only killed two and captured seventeen. The rest, including Bryson, escaped into the woods. I sent Lieutenant Taylor with some Cherokees to run him down. They followed the tracks of two horses right to Bryson's own house. At the house, they ordered Bryson to stop, but he did not, and they shot him to pieces. Later some of my Indians were seen dressed in parts of Bryson's uniform, with his blood still on them. If he had not been killed, he would have been a likely candidate for this place."

"I believe that you're right about all that, Colonel Thomas," said George. He usually said mister rather than colonel, but all this talk of the War Between the States had infused in him a sudden admiration for Colonel Thomas. George was a good Southern boy and was nostalgic for the Confederacy. "And Colonel Thomas, I do love to hear you tell about the war."

Wil chuckled. "I believe they scalped him," he said.

"Really?"

"Yes. I would have burned his house down as well."

"You should have ridden out with your men," said George.

"Yes, I really ought to have gone with them."

Wil finished his pipe and knocked the dottle out of the bowl. He dropped the still hot pipe back into his coat pocket. "I'd better get back inside," said George. Wil looked toward a small table with four chairs around it that was standing under a large shade tree off to his left.

"Can I sit out here for a while?" he asked.

"Of course," said George, and he took out his tobacco pouch and a match and offered them to Wil. Wil took them, refilled his pipe bowl, and then handed the pouch back. "Thank you," he said.

"You're welcome," said George. He turned and headed back into the building. Wil walked to the table and sat down in one of the chairs to smoke his pipe. It was very pleasant. He could not recall many times around this madhouse that were as pleasant as this. He puffed and then he watched the smoke as it rose high and dissipated, seeming to rise up to join with the puffy white clouds overhead. He recalled lessons from old Yonaguska, and he decided that he should be making a prayer with his smoke.

CHAPTER SEVENTEEN

The Prayer

"You up there, high up above, this is Wil Usdi talking to you, sending you my words with this good tobacco. Hear my words. I've not spoken to you for a long spell now. For that I apologize. I want to thank you for my good life, for all the successes I've had—in business, in the government, in the army, with the Cherokee people. I thank you for my good mother, my good wife, and all my good children. I don't know why they don't come to see me in this place where I am now confined, but still I thank you for them. Oh, yes, my mother and my good wife are dead and gone, I believe.

"I thank you for my long life, but I now think that it has been long enough. I am ready to leave this place and go up on high to live with you, to see my mother and my wife again. Perhaps I'll even get to see my father for the first time, and old Yonaguska. Maybe I'll see him again, good old Yonaguska. They have taken away all my weapons, so I have no way to do away with myself. I ask you to take me away, to take me unto yourself. I beg you to do that. I want to go now. I thank you for being with me all this long time, and I hope I have not tried your patience by hanging around here so long. I apologize to you for my madness, although I believe that I have had no control of it. Take me now. Sgi. Yu."

Then he thought, I forgot to thank him for letting me kill Bryson, the damned Tory. But maybe it would not have been right for me to thank the Creator for a killing. I don't know. Now that I have prayed for it, maybe he will take my life away. God, I hope so. If not, perhaps he'll show me where my weapons are hidden, so that I may do myself in. I'm so tired of all this, of this place, of my recurring madness. I'm tired of it all. I want to know how old I am.

As he puffed smoke into the heavens, he fantasized about discovering his weapons. He imagined holding his sword and turning it backward with the point at his belly and then falling on it like an old Roman. If he could not find it, perhaps he would find his knife. He could slice his own throat, but that did not seem very certain. Then he considered his revolver. He could hold it pointed up, just under his chin, and pull the trigger, sending the ball straight up and out through the top of his head. That was more like it. That seemed quick and certain.

He wondered if George would help him. He could ask George to find him a revolver and smuggle it in to him. No one would find out. There would be no one left alive to tell. He decided he would ask George at his next opportunity. George was a good man, especially good for someone who worked in this horrible madhouse. Surely George would help him out in that small way. He should have given thanks in his prayer for good old George.

Wil had another couple of bad days, and then he had a wonderful surprise. George came into his room. "Mr. Thomas, I have a buggy and horse and permission from the boss. Would you care to go out for a buggy ride today? It's a beautiful day today."

"Why, yes. Thank you, George."

Wil Usdi put on his tie and jacket and a top hat, and he walked out the front door of the building with George. The buggy was standing there waiting, and the two of them climbed in. George whipped up the horse, and they trotted off down the lane that led out of the front gate. Wil Usdi thrilled to the feel of the wind in his face. Now and then he had to raise a hand to hold his hat on. He took great delight in recognizing the homes of people he knew, or had known, and it was always a thrill to him to see the horses and cattle grazing in the fields they passed by. But the greatest feeling of all was from watching the constantly changing views of the distant mountains, sometimes five layers of mountain ranges within view.

He said a silent prayer to *Jul'calla*, the ruler over all this mountain land and over all the creatures who lived in the mountains. *Jul'calla*, known in English as Judaculla, the Slant-eyed Giant. Wil Usdi imagined him perched high on one of the far mountain crests puffing on a pipe and sending out smoke that formed the hovering mists that gave the name to the Smoky Mountains.

The buggy hit a bump and then slid toward the edge of the road. George managed to keep control, but Wil wondered why the state legislature was so negligent. He thought back to the time when he had served in that august body and had presented legislation to pave the roads in the western part of the state. And then he, himself, had gone out with the road crews and helped to lay the planks that gave the roads their first pavement. They had laid two long planks down like wagon tracks and then laid out split logs crossways, their round sides down, and tacked them to the planks. It was like a wooden railroad track with the iron rails being the planks and the ties then being laid on top instead of under the tracks. But the ties were laid close together and were what would be ridden on.

However, after several seasons of many wet and rainy days, the boards would begin to disintegrate and rot and the logs would separate. The road would need to be repaired. This one they were riding on desperately needed repairs. For a moment,

Wil thought that he could once again lead such a crew and work with them, but that thought did not last long. His legs were hurting him at the moment, and he knew that he would not be able to last even an hour at such labor. Still he wished that a crew could be sent out to do the job.

They drove past a field of tobacco, and Wil took note of the black slaves at work. "But no," he said in a hushed voice that even George could not hear, "they are not slaves any more. They are free men, and the owner of the place must pay them to work." Times had certainly changed. He wondered how old he might be.

After a drive of an hour or so, George took Wil back to the building at Morganton and walked him back into his cell. Wil thanked George kindly for his courtesy. He took off his hat and coat and tie and sat down in his chair. George went on his way.

Wil sat and stared at the window. He did not really have much of a view out the window, only the yard outside and the fence, a slight rise of the ground beyond the fence, a few trees and a couple of houses. A grazing horse wandered occasionally in front of one of the houses. He thought of the beautiful views of mountains he had enjoyed on his recent ride with George. He wondered what he would see if he should die. It was about time for him to die, he thought. Actually, his death was long overdue. He tried to call to mind anyone he knew who was still alive. He could not think of anyone. They had all left him some time ago. He was alone except for a few kind young people like George.

He got up and walked over to his bed. He stretched himself out on the bed. His legs hurt. He stared straight up at the ceiling. His vision blurred. He saw a vast green field and in the distance a forest. He walked toward the trees until he came close and noticed a path through them. He made his way onto the path, and he was in almost total darkness because of the heavy canopy of branches. The strange thing, though, was the light along the path. At the far end it was very bright. He saw some figures there, just standing as if they were waiting for something. He walked faster. His legs did not hurt.

When he approached the end of the path his heart thrilled, for he thought he could see his mother standing there. He hurried to her. She was smiling and waiting with outstretched arms. What a joy. He embraced her and tears ran down his cheeks. Then over her shoulder he could see his Sarah waiting. How long had they been standing there waiting for him? He did not know, of course, but he hurried to Sarah. He had longed for her embrace for so long now, for so many lonely years, and what a relief it was to hold her once again.

Yonaguska waited a respectable amount of time before interrupting the lovers' reunion. He held out a hand for Wil Usdi, and Wil accepted it greedily. "Wil Usdi," the old man said with a broad smile on his face, "we all knew you were coming, so we waited here for you, and what a great pleasure it is to see you again."

The vision faded to blackness. Wil sat up and strained to bring it back. Then he gasped, and all the strength seemed to drain from his body. He went suddenly limp, and he fell back on the bed, the life at last gone from his long-suffering body.